The Mines of Venus

The
Mines
of
Venus

DAVID WARD

OLIVER
NELSON

THOMAS NELSON PUBLISHERS
Nashville • Atlanta • London • Vancouver

Published in Nashville, Tennessee, by Thomas Nelson, Inc., Publishers, and distributed in Canada by Word Communications, Ltd., Richmond, British Columbia.

The Bible version used in this publication is THE NEW KING JAMES VERSION. Copyright © 1979, 1980, 1982, Thomas Nelson, Inc., Publishers.

Library of Congress Cataloging-in-Publication Data

Ward, David, 1961–
    The mines of Venus / David Ward.
        p.   cm. — (Perimeter One adventure series ; bk. 4)
    Summary: Having run into a ruthless plot to seize control of the mining colony they are visiting on Venus, the Grahams take refuge with underground dwellers who have been secretly practicing Christianity.
    ISBN 0-8407-9238-7 (pbk.)
    [1. Science fiction.   2. Christian life—Fiction.]   I. Title.
II. Series: Ward, David, 1961–   Perimeter One adventure series ; bk. 4.
PZ7.W1873Mh   1994
[Fic]—dc20
                                                            94–16040
                                                               CIP
                                                                AC

Printed in the United States of America.

1 2 3 4 5 6 — 99 98 97 96 95 94

Prologue

The tunnel was dark and foreboding, the air stale and rank with the smell of death. Hewn from solid rock over a century earlier, the tunnel had seen the passage of few mortal men because of the tales of horror regarding the creature that lived in the chamber at the end.

So it was with some fear and trepidation that the two robed and hooded men made their way along in the darkness. The tunnel had little ventilation, so torches could not be used. The only light in the passageway was from the unholy red glow up ahead.

They rounded the corner and stopped at the entrance to a large chamber. The stench was overpowering now, the floor littered with animal carcasses and worse. Shelves cut into the wall held a mass of oozing jars and bottles, and in the middle of the room, on an altar of stones, stood a wide silver bowl.

Flames from beneath the stones heated the bowl so that it glowed with an eery light, and foul vapors roiled out onto the floor. Behind the altar crouched an old hag of a woman with stringy gray hair and a milky white film in the sockets where her eyes should have been. She leaned through the putrid fog and hissed at the two intruders.

Involuntarily they took a step back, but then bowed low and removed their hoods. The taller of the two men had fair hair and a beard, and the other had dark hair and a rugged, tan complexion. The dark one had roughened hands, like one who works with stone. Neither man dared to speak.

"How dare you disturb me in my lair?" the hag shrieked.

The dark one looked up and forced his tongue to move. "F-f-forgive us, Seer. We had no intention to surprise you."

The milky, unseeing eyes narrowed to slits, and the Seer's lips peeled away from her teeth in a predatory grin. "You cannot surprise me. I knew you were coming before you did. Now state your purpose!"

"You told us the time would be soon, yet still we wait. The people are losing courage."

The hag snarled and grabbed a vial from a shelf, pouring it into the bowl. The rancid mixture within emitted a sickly greenish glow. She began to shake, uttering arcane guttural noises that gradually grew to a keening wail. The two men turned to run for their lives, but she began to speak.

"It comes! It comes! Before the harvest it comes to destroy us all!"

This time the fair one spoke. "What is it, Seer? What comes? The harvest is a month away."

"It is a restless evil, full of deadly poison! It comes to banish us to the pit!"

"But what is it? By what name is it called?"

The hag convulsed and spat, as if uttering a curse.

"Graaahaaam!!! It is called by the name of Graham!"

CHAPTER 1

It was summertime in Arlington, Virginia, and the trees were lush and green after the spring rains. The humidity was high, and the mosquitos plentiful. In the muggy heat of the early afternoon sun, a ground car swooped up Arlington Ridge Road and down Twenty-third Avenue, stopping in front of a townhouse on King Street.

The driver's door opened and Dr. Nathan Graham stepped out. He was in his forties, with glasses and a tidy salt-and-pepper mustache. Ordinarily, he would have been hard at work at his job across town at SAFCOM, the largest communications company in the solar system, but today he had the unique pleasure of picking his oldest son up at Washington National Airport.

Chris Graham got out of the passenger side and headed for the back of the car to unload his luggage. He was in his late teens, with sandy brown hair, and had just finished his third year at the Space Sciences Academy on Io, one of Jupiter's moons. With an air of finality, he reached into the trunk and pulled out his bags.

"I still can't believe these made it. Last year, Leigh's bags went to Norway, and she had to buy a whole new wardrobe. Not that she minded, of course." Leigh Quintana was his steady girlfriend at the academy. Her home was in California and they had agreed to meet later in the summer.

It had been a long trip, and Chris was looking forward to

sleeping in his own bed. The flight from Io had taken two weeks by passenger ship, followed by a supersonic transport trip from the spaceport in Australia to New York City. The hop from New York to Washington, D.C., was a short domestic flight, but Chris was exhausted by the time the plane touched down.

They hauled the baggage up to the front door, and Chris rang the doorbell. His mother, Millie, opened the door. She was almost as old as her husband (although she would never admit it in public) and her dark hair was touched with only a few wisps of gray. When she saw who was at the door, she let out a squeal of delight and wrapped her son in her arms. Nathan was completely forgotten for the moment, but he didn't mind one bit. He was as happy to see their son as she was.

With a little help from Millie, father and son moved the bags into the house and closed the door. Chris looked around to be sure that everything was pretty much the way it had been the last time he was home. He looked up the stairs.

"Where are the runts?"

"Amie's over at a friend's house. Ryan is still at work."

"Where's he working?"

"He has a construction job downtown. He's added a few muscles—I'd think twice before I called him a runt."

Chris laughed at that. He reached over to carry his bags upstairs when his dad's communicator beeped. Nathan grimaced and answered the call.

"Nathan Graham. You're kidding—now? But you know my son just . . . yes . . . yes . . . fine. I'll be there in half an hour."

Millie looked at her husband with a sympathetic expression. "Back to work?"

Nathan shook his head in disgust. "I can't believe they couldn't leave me alone for one afternoon. There's an emergency meeting of all department heads. I have to be there. I'm really sorry, Chris."

Chris smiled and shrugged. "That's okay, Dad. We've got all summer."

Nathan cheered up a little, kissed Millie good-bye, and disappeared out the door. Millie stared after him for a moment.

"Dad has a great job, but it does have its down side," Chris observed, starting up the stairs with an armload of bags. Millie followed with as many bags as she could carry. They reached the top of the stairs and crossed the hall to Chris's bedroom. Millie had kept everything exactly as he had left it—only cleaner. They dropped the bags in a heap on the floor.

Chris looked at his mom. "You look thinner. Have you lost weight?"

Millie smiled. "You just remember me fat. Why the flattery? Do you need a loan or something?"

Chris put his hand to his heart. "Mother! You cut me to the quick. You really look thinner to me. But now that you mention it, I would like to borrow the car tonight to track down an old friend or two."

"I'm sure that will be fine."

They retrieved the rest of the bags from the landing by the front door and dragged them up to his room. Millie surveyed the disarray with a sigh.

"You will clean this up right away, won't you?"

"Sure, Mom. I was wondering, how are arrangements going for our little trip out West?"

"Great. Everything's all set."

The Grahams had been planning for some time now to rent a recreational vehicle and drive it cross-country for some sight-seeing. The plan was to finish up in California for an extended visit with some relatives and Leigh Quintana. Chris hadn't seen Leigh for almost three weeks now, and he missed her very much.

"Is Ryan still planning to stay here?" Chris asked.

Millie frowned, disappointed by the thought. "He feels like he has to. He can't very well start a job and then go on vacation for five weeks."

Chris nodded. "Too bad. He's going to miss a great trip."

Ryan Graham stood twelve feet deep in a large pit, working on a wall of concrete and rebar with a sledgehammer. He was two years younger than Chris but tall for his age, with dark hair and an easy smile. Thanks to some accelerated classes when he was younger, he had graduated from high school two years early and decided to work for the summer before heading off to college. He landed the construction job two days after commencement and went right to work.

The project he was working on required the demolition of an existing building before they could begin construction. As the new kid on the job, the other workers had given him a hard time from the outset. And now as a gag, the crew boss had set Ryan to work on a wall with only a sledgehammer, when a wrecking ball would have been more appropriate. Naively Ryan put his back into the work, determined to give it his best effort, even if the task seemed hopeless. He swung the sledgehammer again and again, but only infuriatingly small pieces of concrete chipped off.

In frustration, Ryan put everything he had into one mighty blow, and a large piece of concrete flew out of the wall, hitting him in the arm. He dropped the hammer and grabbed his upper arm, doubled over from the pain.

He looked up to see Mario, a stocky Hispanic fellow, heading his way with a couple of beer cans. "Stand up!" he yelled, speaking with a slight accent.

Ryan did as he was told, and Mario continued. "Make a fist with your right hand and press it into your left as hard and as long as you can."

Ryan did so and the pain got worse at first, then gradually subsided. Mario held out one of the cans. "I brought you a beer."

Ryan smiled. "Thanks, but I don't drink."

"It's non-alcoholic. The foreman doesn't allow liquor on the site."

Ryan took the can, popped the top, and drained it in several long gulps, ignoring the sting of the bubbles as they went down. When the can was empty, he let loose with a burp of Olympian proportions.

"Excuse me."

"That's okay. You gotta keep up your fluids when you work in the heat like this."

Just then, the foreman yelled from the top of the pit. "Hey, Graham! There's a call for you in the trailer!"

Ryan hiked out of the pit and over to the mobile home that served as the office on site. Inside, the room smelled strongly of tobacco smoke. The desk was a disaster area, but he found the communicator without difficulty.

"Ryan Graham."

"Ryan, it's Dad."

"Hi. What's up?"

"You're not going to believe it."

Nathan came home from work just after sunset and called an emergency family meeting in the living room. Millie, Chris, Ryan, and Amie—who was three years younger than Ryan—waited expectantly as Nathan cleared his throat. Everyone but Ryan was mystified; Nathan was giddy with excitement. He didn't know how his family was going to react to his news. He opened the meeting with a prayer for guidance and then looked around the room.

"Ryan, why don't you tell us what you did today?" Nathan said at last.

"I quit my job."

Millie was appalled. "You quit your job? Whatever for?"

Nathan leaned forward in his chair, unable to contain himself any longer.

"We're going to Venus!"

The response from his family could not have been more dramatic if he said he was going to rob a bank.

"This is a joke, right?" Chris asked.

Millie was trying to be open-minded. "Venus? But Nathan, our trip to California—our plans?"

Amie just said, "Cool!" and grinned at Ryan.

Nathan held up his hand for silence.

"I know, as usual this is terribly sudden. At the staff meeting today they told us that the new colony on Mercury lies in a communication shadow during part of its orbit. In order to establish full-time communications with the colony, SAFCOM is going to try to build a booster station on Venus."

"But why are *we* going?" Chris asked.

"I was drafted to head up the first contact with the Venus colony. Reports have been sporadic and no one knows exactly what the conditions are. They need someone to mediate between the company and the colony. I have to convince them that having a booster station outside their biodomes is a good idea."

Amie looked interested. "What's a biodome?"

"The atmosphere of Venus is pretty hostile. The colonists have to live inside domes to survive. They want me to leave as soon as possible, and since they're messing up our vacation plans, they said I could bring you all along at company expense. There aren't any commercial flights to Venus, and rumor has it that the colonists don't think much of tourists. We may never get another chance like this."

Ryan's ears pricked up. "What if the colony doesn't want us there?"

"Oh, they will. We're getting together a very attractive benefits package for them. Their only industry is a mining company which employs almost the entire community. My guess is they would be glad for an opportunity to expand their business."

Chris frowned. "Oh, no."

"What is it?" Millie asked.

"Leigh. She's going to kill me."

Nathan thought quickly. "Tell her you're just postponing your visit. We'll fly you out for the second half of the summer."

As the original plan had been to spend only a couple of weeks in California, a month and a half sounded pretty good to Chris. He was willing to wager that Leigh, though disappointed at the delay, would agree.

Preliminary negotiations between SAFCOM and the Maddock Mining Company—Terran Division—began the next day. The result was a multimillion-dollar arrangement for community support funds and educational programs for the colony on

Venus, assuming the companies could reach a mutually beneficial agreement.

The mining company expressed an interest in pursuing negotiations and offered to fly the Grahams out. The next shipment was due in seven days, with one day scheduled for refueling and an immediate departure for Venus. The Grahams were booked on the flight.

The ore ship was scheduled to land in Pakistan, so the Grahams made reservations to India, as there were no direct flights to Pakistan. There was less traffic to that part of the globe this time of year because of the heat, so they had no trouble making their reservations only a week in advance.

Nathan warned the family that the accommodations on the barge were likely to be quite primitive, and he had no idea what to expect on Venus. They packed as simply as they could, streamlining their personal effects to one bag each and made arrangements for someone to look after the house while they were gone.

The day of departure felt like the beginning of a vacation, even though Nathan was going to have to work. Everyone's spirits remained high during the three-hour trip to India. Then, on approach to Pakistan they got a good view of the ore ship on an adjacent landing pad.

The *Mother Lode,* as she was called, was a long, bulbous, scabby-looking ship, six-hundred feet long and covered with corrosion from stem to stern.

Chris was curious. "What makes the hull corrode like that? It's not made of iron, is it?"

Nathan looked at the ship thoughtfully for a moment. "The atmosphere of Venus, I suspect. Including some down time for maintenance, they probably spend about a hundred days a year there."

The Grahams exited the transport and walked past a convoy of trucks parked along the perimeter of the landing pad. Workers in white shirts and pants, some wearing wrappings around their heads, ran to and fro, servicing the ship, unloading the last truckloads of sulfur, and performing other miscellaneous duties.

With Nathan in the lead, they approached a burly man in a flight jacket standing by the loading ramp. He looked as if he had neither shaved nor bathed for a week, but Nathan approached him without hesitation.

"Excuse me, sir? I'm looking for the captain."

"Found him, you did," the man said with a peculiar accent. "You are being Nathan Graham."

"I'm afraid you have me at a disadvantage."

"You are not being Nathan Graham?"

"No. I mean, yes, I am Nathan Graham. Who are you?"

"You call me Garushta Fairborne. You I take to the colony."

Nathan found himself nodding. "Yes. You take us to the colony."

The captain grinned and nodded back, saying nothing. Nathan began to feel they weren't getting anywhere. "Can we come aboard?"

"Kum a bord?"

Nathan struggled to put the words in a syntax Captain Fairborne could understand. "You take I up to ship?" He pointed up the ramp for added emphasis.

The captain grinned again and nodded. "Yes, yes, we cross the door."

He walked up the ramp, and his family followed him, trying not to do or say anything insulting. As they passed through the door, the temperature dropped ten degrees, and their eyes took a minute to grow accustomed to the dim lighting inside.

The walls were rust-colored, though not corroded, and there were grimy yellow lights spaced evenly down the passageways. Then they noticed the odor.

"It smells like rotten eggs," Amie said, wrinkling her nose.

"That's the sulfur they're transporting, sweetheart," Nathan replied quietly.

The captain led them down a long passageway, finally stopping in front of a grubby little room strewn with blankets and crates. Nathan began to realize, with increasing distaste, that the

8

crates had been arranged to provide sleeping accommodations.

"You don't mean to put all of us in here?" Nathan asked, as politely as possible.

The captain looked a bit confused and then gave up trying to understand and waved his arm. "You here stay. All rooms full."

The captain turned perfunctorily and disappeared down the hall, leaving the Grahams to sort the situation out for themselves. They spent a few minutes trying to make the best of the cramped quarters, dividing the blankets so they all had some padding on the crates that would serve as their beds.

"This is definitely not the Ri'anna," Ryan said, referring to a Denver hotel he had stayed in a few months earlier.

Nathan was apologetic. "I didn't expect it to be quite this bad. We can still call it off if you want."

Millie shook her head. "No, we'll be all right. This is a once-in-a-lifetime opportunity, remember?" She still had her sense of humor.

Nathan looked to his children, all of whom were nodding their agreement. "You guys are terrific. I think this is going to be a great trip."

The ship was designed to take off and land in a horizontal position because of the tremendous loads of ore it carried. This meant that in addition to the main thrusters, which were among the most powerful anywhere, the ship was equipped with enormous vertical thrusters. The titanic bulk of the *Mother Lode* made launching such a lumbering, gradual process that of all the seats on the ship, only the pilots' chairs were equipped with restraining straps.

The Grahams made themselves as comfortable as they could during takeoff, sitting on the blankets and holding onto the tops of the crates and some of the nearest bulkheads. Once the ship blasted out of orbit, they discussed what their next activity ought to be. An unguided tour of the vessel didn't sound like a good idea, but the thought of just sitting in the room was intolerable. Nathan finally decided to do some detective work and see what he could find out.

After a few minutes of wandering around the passageways, he ran into one of the crew members. Several awkward attempts at conversation produced only a blank stare, and the man finally said something completely unintelligible and left. Nathan continued his expedition until he encountered another crewman.

"Excuse me?"

"Veh?" the crewman said.

"I'm looking for the captain."

The crewman looked bewildered, and then realization swept over his face. "Fairborne?"

"Yes, yes, I'm looking for Captain Fairborne."

"Ja vis tra meh," the crewman replied, indicating that Nathan should follow him.

They wound through the passages until Nathan was utterly lost, coming to a stop before a cabin indistinguishable from all the others they had walked past. The crewman knocked on the door and a moment later, the captain appeared. He looked annoyed at the crewman for the interruption, then he noticed Nathan. He dismissed the crewman with a wave of his hand.

"Doctor Graham. Help you need?"

Nathan caught a glimpse of the captain's cabin over Fairborne's shoulder, and his complaint about their accommodations died on his lips. It appeared that the captain would be sleeping on crates as well. Several cardboard boxes were scattered about the room, containing an assortment of manifests, rosters, and inventory sheets. Across from the makeshift bed was a desk also made out of crates.

Nathan thought quickly to come up with a more suitable line of inquiry. "We were wondering where you eat, and what you have in the way of . . . lavatory facilities."

He did not have much hope that the captain would understand him, and his doubt was confirmed by the look on the captain's face. Plunging into a mixture of humiliating gestures and sounds, Nathan managed to communicate his concern to the captain, who burst out laughing.

"You with me come."

Nathan was escorted through the hallways once more, finally ending up back where he had started. Millie and the children looked expectantly at the captain, and he conveyed via hand gestures that the entire family should accompany him.

Hopes for better accommodations were dashed, when a short walk down the hall brought them to the filthy, smelly room that served as the latrine for their section of the ship. Millie strained mentally to find something good about the facilities and decided that she was thankful that the stalls had doors. The captain led them back to their room and made as if to speak, but paused as he searched for words.

"The . . . uh . . . the cake . . . uh . . . cook, the cook your food to you."

Nathan had to mentally break the sentence up before he understood. "The cook will bring the food here?"

"The food here, yes." The captain smiled, nodded, and was gone.

Ryan was incredulous. "Who are these guys?"

Nathan shook his head. "I have no idea. I heard one of the crew speak in their native language, I think. I've been all over the world, and I couldn't identify it."

Amie sat down on a blanket. "The captain seems nice enough."

"I suspect he was instructed by his superiors to treat us well," Nathan replied. "An association with SAFCOM could mean a hefty profit for the mining company."

Chris stretched out on his crate. "On the way to the airport this morning, you told us the main offices for the Maddock Mining Company were on Venus. Do you suppose the crew members are from the colony?"

Nathan snapped his fingers. "That has to be it. But the colonists originated from Earth only a hundred fifty years ago. How could they develop their own language so quickly?"

No one had an answer, so Millie changed the subject. "Nathan, what are we going to do for the next week and a half?

There are no recreational facilities, and I doubt the crew wants us poking about."

Nathan looked around the room with resignation. "I guess we'll stay here. I hope everyone brought something to read."

The trip on the ore ship seemed one of the longest any of them could remember. They played games, talked, wrote, read—anything they could think of to pass the time. Each day began with a prayer and breakfast, followed by whatever activity they could conjure up. After the first few hours of sitting around, Nathan decided he had better lead the group in some calisthenics every hour or so, just to protect their muscles from atrophy.

Sleeping was difficult at first because of the hardness of the crates, but the blankets were quite soft, which made the situation tolerable. With the lights out and everyone quiet, the gentle thrumming of the engines created a soothing backdrop, which made it easier to fall asleep.

By the end of four days, everyone had finished reading everyone else's books, and they were running out of things to do. Chris came up with a game wherein he would be the "computer" and Ryan and Amie would choose characters, give them attributes, and then embark on a quest to save an imaginary kingdom. Once they got the hang of it, they were able to spend long hours at it, and before long, Millie wanted to play, too.

Chris sat with his back against a crate. "Okay. You're standing at the edge of a round pool, filled with dark, murky water. In the center of the pool is an obsidian dais with an altar of shimmering blue opal. There is an amber gemstone on top. There is a rowboat here."

Ryan closed his eyes, trying to picture the scene. "I want to get in the boat."

Amie shook her head. "No way. You know he's just going to kill us again."

Chris laughed. "You always have a chance. There's always a way to win."

Millie made a decision. "I'll get in the boat with Ryan."

Chris thought for a moment, trying to imagine how the action might unfold. "Okay. The queen and the knight get in the boat. Fearing the unknown, the prophet stays on the shore with her bow at ready. You row halfway to the dais, when the queen happens to look over the side. Directly below the boat is an eyeball three feet across."

"Told ya," Amie said smugly.

Millie looked a little frantic. "Go back! Go back!"

Chris continued. "In a fit of panic, the queen grabs the oars away from the knight and starts paddling furiously. You have gone only a few feet when the water behind the boat erupts in an explosion of spray. A huge black dragon rises up out of the pool."

"I want to use my sword," Ryan said.

"You swing, but the dragon is out of reach. Your follow-through nearly decapitates the queen."

Ryan turned to his mom. "Sorry."

Millie looked at Amie. "Use your bow."

Amie thought for a moment. "I want to pray before I shoot."

Chris was silent again for a moment. "The prophet utters a sincere prayer to the living God for His gracious help in their time of need. She fits an arrow to the string and pulls back, closing her eyes. With one last prayer, she lets fly. The arrow makes a magnificent arc through the air and an angel swoops down from the heavens, guiding the arrow straight and true into the heart of the beast. With a final gasp, the dragon slips beneath the dark waters."

The game went on like this for some time. At one point, Nathan joined them as the king, but he asked too many questions and eventually the other characters sent the king to the "land where kings are eternally blessed," and Nathan went back to his reading file.

The pleasant surprise was the food. On their first morning the Grahams were expecting something stale and moldy, with brackish water. Astonishingly, breakfast consisted of thin, rare strips of beef, served with bread, fruit, and freshly squeezed orange juice. They assumed breakfast to be a lucky accident, until the rickety cart appeared again at midday.

Lunch was beef stew and corn bread, with fresh whole milk. Dinner was best of all: steaks with an assortment of vegetables and bread, and some sort of ale. The meals were the same, delivered three times every day by one of the crew, but the food was so delicious that no one grew tired of it.

One afternoon, after a brief stop by the latrine, Chris decided he could no longer bear the thought of going back to their little room. He decided to risk an unguided tour of the ship.

Not wishing to get lost—the thought of trying to wring directions out of a crewman was not very appealing—he chose to keep his path simple. He headed down the nearly featureless hallway, passing identical doors with some frequency. Every fifty feet or so there was a side passage leading off to the left. He walked past the first two and tried the third.

The passage fed into another hallway, short enough to see either end from where he was standing. Thirty feet to the right was a door, different from the doors to the crew cabins. A brief examination of the controls for the door revealed that there was no security. He pushed the button, and the door slid open into the wall.

Chris had expected almost any other sight than the one that met his eyes. The room was huge, and the floor was covered with soil and grass. Dozens of cows were grazing on real grass in a meadow near the center of the room. Environmental controls along the walls and ceiling carefully modulated the temperature and humidity. Now he knew why the food was so good.

He turned to go and was suddenly face to face with one of the crewmen. This rotund fellow was anything but jocular. His face flushed red, and his mouth spluttered a vehement reprimand, of which Chris understood not a single word. He got the gist, though. This place was the round fellow's responsibility, and if this stupid foreigner from Earth didn't have better manners than this, he could jolly well starve.

Chris beat a hasty retreat and hurried back to the guest quarters. Once he told the family about his little excursion, it was

14

decided unanimously that they would stay put for the remainder of the journey, no matter how excruciatingly dull the voyage was.

With one day to go, Nathan tracked down Captain Fairborne and spent fifteen minutes trying to explain to him that the whole family wanted to see Venus when the ship was coming in to land. Reluctantly, the captain acquiesced. The following afternoon, the family was ushered into the command center at the front of the ship.

The command center was constructed of a material different from the rest of the ship, as if someone knew when to be thrifty and when to invest in the best. Several consoles of the latest technology available adorned the walls, and the pilots sat before a complicated array of buttons and navigational equipment. The captain walked up behind the pilots.

"Tera sey too vat elend deshift."

The pilots nodded but neither turned nor acknowledged the Grahams's presence in any way. The view of the stars out the front window was beautiful; the sun pale and far to the side. As they watched, a small dot in the distance gradually began to grow until they could see it was a planet.

Venus was sometimes referred to as Earth's sister planet. It was about the same size, with a surface of basalt and an assortment of common elements and minerals. The atmosphere was composed of carbon dioxide, however, instead of oxygen and nitrogen. Dense clouds reflected much of the sun's light, but the small amount of heat that was trapped near the surface created temperatures close to 900 degrees Fahrenheit, which made the planet uninhabitable for humans. Though it was the second planet from the sun, Venus was actually hotter than Mercury, the planet closest to the sun.

For reasons no scientist could explain outside of random chance, the planet Venus rotated "backward" in comparison to the Earth's rotation, and very slowly. The Venusian day was 114 Earth hours long, while the planet's rotation around the sun—hence, the length of its year—was only 225 Earth days. The multilayered blanket of clouds shrouding the planet had the same reverse rotation, but circled the planet once every four days.

From space, Venus was rather nondescript, covered by grayish clouds. The surface of the planet was not visible, even from orbit. As the *Mother Lode* dropped down into the clouds, the pilots watched their instruments intently. Mist began collecting on the outside of the window. Several miles down, they emerged from one layer of clouds and had a brief view of the next layer, similar to the view from a high-flying aircraft on Earth.

After a few minutes of blind flying through the next thick layer of carbon dioxide clouds, the mist became droplets, and rain pelted the window. Seeing something so familiar this far from home was a comforting sight.

"Oh! It's rain!" Amie said, as if she had discovered buried treasure.

Nathan put his hand on her shoulder. "Those are drops of sulfuric acid, *Liebchen*."

Amie was taken aback. "Oh."

The ship continued its descent, finally dropping through the last layer of clouds fifteen miles above the surface. The scene below was not unlike a vista from Earth, only completely devoid of life. There were mountains without greenery, valleys without trees, deeps without water, no microbes, no bacteria, not even amino acids—utterly lifeless.

The *Mother Lode* came in low over the mountains, losing speed and altitude until the ship hovered over one of three large domes set into the side of some low foothills. Nearby a rough plain stretched on for miles. The pilots maneuvered the ship through a gigantic opening in the dome below and landed on an expansive pad inside. The opening in the dome closed overhead, and the landing bay filled with air.

With a wave of thanks to Captain Fairborne, the Grahams walked quickly back to their room to retrieve their baggage. They were eager to move on to different surroundings. They found the way out, and soon they were walking down the ramp with Nathan in the lead.

As they descended from the ship, Chris noticed that the entire crew was busy with the unloading process. The launch bay was double the size of a football stadium, built to accommodate ore ships the size of the *Mother Lode*.

They crossed the fifty feet to the exit doors and were met by three men in business suits. The leader looked to be in his late fifties or early sixties but sporting a full head of black hair. He had broad shoulders and an engaging smile, which he flashed as he held out his hand.

Nathan shook the proffered hand. "Doctor Nathan Graham."

"Halton Maddock. This is my son, Brice."

Brice Maddock was well-built and handsome like his father, but as he shook Nathan's hand, his smile never quite reached his eyes.

"Nice to meet you, Brice."

Halton Maddock continued. "And this is Samuel Vile. He will be the representative for the colony during negotiations."

Sammy Vile was around forty, with matted brown hair and a smile that was missing a few teeth. He gave the appearance of a former bum, now washed and stuffed into a suit that was a little too big for him. Nathan smiled anyway and shook his hand.

"Pleased to meet you, Mr. Vile."

"Likewise."

Nathan introduced Millie and the children, and the group exchanged pleasantries until Halton Maddock waved his hand toward the exit doors.

"Welcome to Venus, all of you. If you'll come with me, I'll show you to your quarters."

The doors opened automatically as the group approached, and they passed through the doors into a concrete antechamber full of huge, egg-shaped containers. Two dozen sat on racks to one side. The only exits appeared to be large tunnels at either end of the room.

Chris was curious. "Are these shipping containers?"

Halton walked over to one of the rack-mounted containers and opened it up. Inside was a seat with a simple control panel

17

in front of it, consisting of a numeric key pad, a red button, a green button, and a map with numbered locations.

"Other than walking," Halton began, "this is our only mode of transportation inside the biodomes. Just key in the number of your destination, push the green button, and you're off. We call them *tube cars,* and you will see why in a few moments. Mr. Vile, would you demonstrate?"

Sammy climbed into the open vehicle, pushed "1" for the Administration Building, and pressed the green button. The canopy closed automatically, sealing Sammy inside, and some machinery under the floor came to life, conveying the tube car over and down into a tile-covered depression which ran the length of the floor between the two tunnels.

As the car came to rest, floating over the metallic tiles, there was a tremendous rush of air out of one tunnel. Sammy's tube car was carried along with increasing speed, and when it reached the entrance to the tunnel, the car took off like a shot. After a few moments, the flow of air shut off and the wind died down.

Halton Maddock beamed. "It runs on the same principle as the EMAG trains on Earth. Since the electromagnets afford a nearly frictionless ride, it doesn't take much air pressure to pull the cars along. Who's next?"

Ryan's hand shot up, and Halton helped him into the next car. The seat was very comfortable, but the firm handles on either side made Ryan feel as if he were on an amusement park ride. He pushed the "1" on the keypad, held his breath, and pressed the green button. The canopy closed overhead and the car moved sideways into the track leading to the tunnel.

The car glided toward the opening up ahead. When the nose of the vehicle entered the tunnel, there was a surge of acceleration, and Ryan was pushed back against his seat. He grabbed the handles with both hands, and for several seconds he could see the translucent inner surface of the tube racing past.

Because of the sudden acceleration, Ryan estimated his speed at ninety to one hundred miles per hour, although in reality it was closer to sixty. After several seconds of light, it was dark again briefly, and then the light changed.

The car slowed to a stop and the canopy opened, revealing a dome constructed of marble walls and vaulted ceilings. Sammy Vile stood beside the track and watched Ryan struggle to extricate himself from the car, but he made no move to help.

"That was some ride," Ryan said, trying to make conversation.

"You get used to it," Sammy replied without emotion.

Millie's car arrived next, followed by Amie, Nathan, Chris, and the Maddocks. The tube car loading area was the lowest level of the Administration Building. As the Grahams followed their hosts they had the sense of being in a modern office building. It soon became apparent as they passed several open doorways that the building was full of apartments as well as offices.

They stopped in front of a locked door, and Halton slipped a plastic card into the designated slot. The door slid open to reveal an enormous, tastefully decorated suite. Plush, light blue carpet stretched across the floor, and the best modern furniture money could buy was positioned tastefully around the room.

On the far side of the living room, a short hallway led to three bedrooms, each with a pair of queen-sized beds. Tucked away to the other side they caught a glimpse of a dining table and galley kitchen. After their accommodations on the ore ship, the Grahams couldn't help feeling as if they had died and gone to heaven.

Halton handed the card key to Nathan. "I hope the room is suitable."

"Oh, yes. Very. Thank you very much," Nathan replied, smiling appreciatively.

Halton continued, "I have scheduled a tour for later this afternoon, so you can be somewhat familiar with our facilities prior to our first meeting tomorrow morning."

Nathan thanked the Maddocks and Sammy Vile for their hospitality and then the three men left quickly, the door closing automatically behind them. Halton stopped in the hallway to address his son.

"Brice, we have a meeting in fifteen minutes. Are you coming with me?"

"I want to walk Sammy to the tube platform, but I'll be at the meeting."

Halton nodded and walked away. Brice had been spending a lot of time with Sammy lately—maybe too much. Still, it was good to keep up relations with the townspeople. He shrugged his shoulders and headed for the elevators to the upper levels, focusing on the agenda for his next meeting.

Sammy and Brice started to retrace their steps to the tube platform, but abruptly Brice pulled Sammy aside into an empty hallway.

"Are you all set for tomorrow?"

Sammy looked around instinctively to be sure that no one was listening. "Yeah. I got two men down shaft number six."

"The meeting starts at nine in the morning. I want him out of there at ten after, for at least fifteen minutes. And we agreed, no one dies."

Sammy nodded. "No one dies."

"Good. Now go and get your people ready for the tour. I'm sorry we didn't know sooner. I should have guessed my father would do something like this. I'll keep them here as long as I can."

Sammy looked around once more, but the hall was empty. He walked quickly down the hall toward the tube platform without looking back. Brice watched him go and then remembered his meeting. He dashed in the opposite direction for the elevator, hoping the next twenty-four hours would go according to plan. With a little luck, by this time tomorrow the company would be his.

CHAPTER 2

The Grahams unpacked their bags leisurely, luxuriating in the expansive comfort afforded by their new accommodations. There were two large bathrooms with wide bathtubs, a fully stocked kitchen, a wide-screen video player with a substantial library of disks, and several computer terminals for accessing a plethora of reading material.

They enjoyed themselves so thoroughly that it seemed only a short time later that Brice Maddock arrived at their door for the tour. He walked them through the dormitory levels of the building, explaining that the employees who worked in the building also lived there. It had been that way ever since the dome was constructed by his great-grandfather.

The tour of the Administration Building finished with Brice's office on the sixth floor. The view was spectacular. Someone had done a marvelous job of Terraforming—making a hostile environment look like Earth. At the edge of the horizon was a huge mountain sprinkled with groves of trees, dwellings, and what appeared to be mine entrances. At the bottom of the hill was a quaint little town where the miners lived. Unfortunately, the otherwise beautiful vista was ruined by the gray, un-Earthly light filtering through the atmosphere of Venus, and the translucent dome overhead.

Brice invited the Grahams to make themselves comfortable, while he filled them in on the history of the settlement. His office was equipped with two sofas and a number of chairs, decorated with elegant taste.

"One hundred and sixty years ago, my great-grandfather, Terrence Maddock, decided he wanted to found a colony on Venus. He convinced the government to accept his proposal to bring twelve hundred colonists to the planet and set up a mining operation that would sustain the community. With governmental approval in hand, he gathered a group of capital investors to finance the operation, and hired an EE and T—Environmental Engineering and Terraforming—company to go ahead of the colonists and build the domes."

Nathan pursed his lips. "That must have been quite an undertaking."

Brice nodded. "Construction took five years and almost every penny he had. There are three domes, counting this one. The dome you landed in is, of course, the spaceport. This dome is devoted to housing and mining operations. The third is used for agriculture and animal husbandry. The colony is entirely self-sufficient. We grow all our own food, and no one ever goes hungry."

"I would think with such an abundant supply of carbon dioxide just outside the dome, growing plants would be a cinch," Chris observed.

"That's right. Twice a day we pump carbon dioxide into the agricultural dome through hundreds of filtering units which remove other gases and particles. The only drawback is the farmers have to wear environment suits."

"Do you have a lot of farmers?"

"Less than fifty. Most of the people work in the mines." For just a moment, Brice looked as if he had said too much.

"Children, too?" Millie asked.

"Of course not, Mrs. Graham. We are not barbarians. Now, if everyone is ready, I think this would be an excellent time to see the town."

It was not lost on Nathan that Brice had changed the subject rather abruptly, and he made a mental note to keep an eye on the younger Mr. Maddock. Brice led them downstairs and out the front door of the Administration Building.

The view that met the Grahams struck them as odd. Instead of a city street, the steps of the building opened onto a dirt path that wound down to the wooded hillside that they had seen from Brice's office. The Grahams followed their host down the path, and it occurred to Nathan again that the scenery would have been beautiful were it not for the sickly, grayish cast of the light from overhead.

The rich, loam soil felt soft underfoot, even though the path was well-travelled. The temperature was quite moderate, but the humidity made everyone feel sticky and slightly irritable. A five-minute walk brought them to the edge of town. There Brice quickly directed them down a side street, explaining that the main thoroughfare was still hazardous due to structural damage from some recent seismic activity.

The view down the side street reminded Chris of pictures from history class of the shanty towns that sprang up during the Great Depression of the 1930s, but something didn't look right. The people were too well-dressed to be living in such squalid shacks, and the vague smiles on their faces made them look as if they were hiding something.

"What are all these nicely dressed people doing in such filthy surroundings?" Chris asked.

Brice attempted a disarming smile but only managed to look as if he had indigestion. "These are only temporary shelters, constructed for the people whose homes were destroyed by the quake."

In a flash Chris knew the man was lying, but he kept his mouth shut. Brice led them down two more streets, each populated by well-dressed people, smiling benignly and wandering nowhere in particular. He explained that there were a few local businesses, specializing in crafts and food stuffs, but most of the wages were earned in the mines.

The tour ended abruptly at the end of the second street, and Brice led them back up the hill to the Administration Building. Nathan said nothing all the way back, but Amie pumped Brice with questions about the children and what they did for recreation. To Millie, Brice's answers seemed evasive; she was beginning to feel uneasy.

By the time Brice dropped them off at their room, it was late afternoon, though the filtered sunlight had not changed in intensity. It would be just as bright as it was when they arrived for many days to come.

Brice reminded Nathan of their meeting at nine o'clock the following morning and bid everyone good night. Nathan closed the door to their suite, listening carefully for receding footfalls in the hall, and then turned and called a family conference.

"I'd like to get everyone's impressions of what we've seen so far," he said casually, dropping into one of the large easy chairs.

Chris sat down on the sofa, poised for action. "Well, for starters, Brice was lying."

Nathan smiled approvingly. "You noticed it, too?"

Chris nodded. "Those buildings weren't damaged by any seismic activity. They were poorly constructed."

"I got a good, close look at one of the structures. The pieces look as old as the dome itself."

"Did you notice the people? They looked like actors on a stage," Millie added from a corner chair.

Not wanting to be left out, Amie jumped in. "I don't think any of them were for real."

Nathan was interested. "Why do you say that?"

"The phony smiles, for one thing. When one of the ladies walked by, I noticed a split in her dress, and she had another dress on underneath."

Nathan paused thoughtfully. "The question that remains to be answered, then, is *Why?*"

Unfortunately, no one had an answer to that. One by one, Amie, Chris, and Ryan found something to distract them in the suite. Millie prepared dinner in the well-stocked kitchenette, and Nathan turned to his notes for the meeting in the morning. One thing was certain—he had some serious questions for Brice Maddock.

* * *

The next morning, Nathan's travel alarm went off at six-thirty, and the Grahams began their day. The refrigerator was well stocked, and Millie enlisted Chris's help in fixing breakfast, while the others took turns in the bathroom. When Nathan was ready, he took over for Chris in the kitchen. Walking up behind his wife, he put his arms around her and kissed her on the neck.

"Good morning."

Millie smiled and tried not to drop the egg she was holding. "Good morning. All ready for your meeting?"

"I think so. I just wish I knew what was going on around here."

Millie whipped the eggs in the pan with a fork. "You'll find out soon enough."

"You know what I miss? The sunrise. You realize how much you count on it when you have to do without it for a while."

Millie nodded. "I think we'll all be ready to go when the time comes to leave."

Nathan had several pieces of French toast going when Ryan walked in a few minutes later. "Okay, Mom. It's your turn."

Millie handed Ryan a fork and pointed to a pan full of sizzling bacon. "These will be ready to flip in about half a minute."

"Mom, I know how to make bacon," he protested.

"You know how to *eat* bacon," Millie replied as she disappeared down the hall.

Breakfast was served at seven-thirty, and the Grahams were ready to walk out the door well before nine. The negotiations had been scheduled in a conference room upstairs, and Nathan felt it was inappropriate for the family to attend. As he gathered up his briefcase he asked them to poke around quietly and see what they could find out.

Standing by the door, they held hands and thanked the Lord for the day, asking Him for safety wherever they went and for success in the negotiations. A short walk down the hall brought them to the elevator, and everyone but Nathan got off on the ground floor. There was a security station nearby, so Millie chose her words very carefully.

"Amie and I are going to take a tour of the building. Want to come along?"

Chris caught the edge in his mom's voice immediately. "Thanks, but I think we'll go for a stroll through town and take in some of the local color."

The words sounded awkward, and Ryan gave his brother an odd look. Millie smiled cheerily and glanced toward the building guard.

"Want to meet back here for lunch?"

Chris nodded. "Sounds good. See you later."

Millie and Amie turned and walked down the nearest hallway, while Ryan and Chris headed out the front door.

"I don't think I'll ever get used to walking out of an office building straight onto a dirt path," Ryan said, shaking his head.

"You gotta admit, it's not like any place we've ever been before."

Ryan smiled wryly. "That much is certain."

They walked down the trail until they were about a hundred feet from town, at which point Chris grabbed Ryan's shoulder and they stopped. They could barely see the main street through the trees, but Chris found himself whispering anyway.

"We've had the official tour. Let's try something different."

He looked both ways along the path, then strode off into the underbrush with Ryan close behind.

Nathan found the conference room with some searching and directions from a helpful employee. When he walked in, Sammy Vile and Brice Maddock were already there, and the three men made small talk until Halton Maddock arrived five minutes later.

"Sorry I'm late. I had a comm conference with some angry union bosses."

"Is everything all right?" Nathan asked.

"Absolutely. They're just griping about conditions in the mines, like they always do. They say one thing, my reports say another. You know union bosses, always pulling for more benefits."

"If we can close this deal, you might be able to provide some," Nathan replied.

Halton smiled broadly. "Agreed. Shall we begin?"

Sammy and Brice nodded, and Nathan spread some documents out on the table in front of them.

"As you know, SAFCOM is interested in building a booster station on Venus to allow nonstop communications between Earth and the new colony on Mercury. We would be saved considerable time and expense if we could build adjacent to your facility, making use of your geotechnical information during the planning process and some of your supplies during construction and operation. In return, we propose to establish a substantial Community Improvement and Education Fund, as well as giving you six percent of net profit for operation of the station."

Halton leaned forward in his seat and folded his hands on the table. "We are intrigued by your offer, Doctor Graham, but there are several items about which we require further. . . ."

He never finished his sentence. A piercing alarm went off somewhere in the building, and a red light began flashing on the communicator mounted in the tabletop in front of him. He punched a button on the control panel.

"This is Maddock. What happened?"

"Shadran in Ops, sir. We have a cave in off shaft number six. Several workers are trapped."

"I'll be right down."

Halton stood up, looking quite concerned. "Excuse me, gentlemen."

Without another word, he turned and walked out of the room. Nathan was surprised by his sudden departure.

"He looked pretty worried."

"Shaft number six is run by the union bosses he was in conference with earlier," Brice explained.

Nathan instinctively understood the delicacy of the situation. "I see. Then he may not be back for some time."

Brice smiled apologetically. "Probably not. As his chief operating officer, I am familiar with your proposal and my father's concerns. We can continue with the meeting if you like, and fill him in on our progress when he gets back."

Something about Brice's aggressiveness made Nathan uncomfortable, but he couldn't argue with the logic. There was no polite way to refuse his host. "Very well."

"Excellent. Now allow me to make a counterproposal. You pay us nine percent of net profits and forget about any funds for community improvement and education. You will end up paying about the same amount, but we can set up the special funds ourselves and administer them here, which will save you a small fortune in administration back home."

Nathan looked at Sammy. "As representative for the people, would you feel comfortable with that arrangement?"

"Oh, yes. Absolutely. We trust the company completely."

Nathan looked intently into the faces of the two men across the table, and knew in that moment that if he agreed to Brice's terms, the townspeople would never see any of the money. Deception was in the air, and Nathan had had enough.

"I'd like to talk to some of the townspeople about it."

Sammy's mouth dropped open, and the look of cocky self-assurance fled Brice's face.

"You can't! I mean . . . it would be inappropriate."

"Why?"

"Because . . . Mr. Vile is the chosen representative of the people, and if you bypass him, you will undermine his authority."

Nathan felt only slightly guilty about watching Brice squirm. "Put it to a vote, then. Let the people decide."

"That is out of the question. There would be rioting. You would throw the town into disorder."

Nathan tried to keep the sarcasm out of his voice.

"Oh, come now. Certainly a society as healthy and well-governed as yours can withstand a little popular vote."

Brice shook his head vehemently. "The concept is foreign to them. I'm afraid I have to forbid it."

"You don't seem to understand, Mr. Maddock. Either I take this issue to the people, or the deal's off."

For just a moment, Brice looked like a trapped animal, but he quickly regained his composure. "Very well, Doctor Graham, since you insist. We can set up a meeting tomorrow."

"Today."

"Today? Doctor Graham, be reasonable!"

"I am being reasonable. I want to meet with the townspeople today, and this time I don't want any sanitized parade of happy faces."

Brice stood up, his own face ashen. "I'll make the arrangements. Mr. Vile, would you accompany me?"

The two men left the room precipitously and headed down the hall to Brice's office. Once they were inside, Brice kicked the door and swore. Looking for an object for his wrath, he pulled several books from the massive library and hurtled them, one by one, across the room. Then he turned savagely on Sammy. Grabbing him by the lapels he threw him up against the wall.

"I have not come this far to be stopped by some pusillanimous maggot from SAFCOM!"

He stormed over to his desk and punched the communicator.

"Security! This is Brice. In half an hour, I want you to round up the family from Earth. Just the mother, two boys, and the girl. Leave the father to me."

Brice terminated the connection and threw his body into his chair, closing his eyes. "Mr. Vile, you will gather the townspeople for an emergency meeting. I want everyone there, including the hag."

Sammy recoiled at the thought of even talking to the Seer. "Saphirra? What do you want her for?"

"For a long time she has prophesied the coming of the Destroyer. Tell her he has arrived and his name is Nathan Graham."

Sammy Vile nodded, his eyes wide, and slipped out of the room. Brice stabbed at the communicator again.

"Dome Three. This is Brice."

"This is Dome Three. Go ahead."

"I'm coming down in ten minutes. I want a demonstration of the filtration system."

"Yes, sir!"

The first floor of the Administration Building was quite ordinary in its assortment and layout of offices, and Millie and Amie found very little of interest until they reached the far left side of the building. At the end of the hallway, glass double doors opened onto an incredibly lush, stunningly beautiful park. A wide path of white stones wandered lazily through a grove of tremendous cherry trees which made a canopy of white blossoms overhead.

Brilliantly colored flower beds lined the path, and wooden benches provided seating here and there throughout the park. The only aspect of the garden which bespoke anything other than outstanding natural beauty was a high wall that ran the perimeter of the park. Coils of barbed wire stood threateningly on top. The sight raised a question immediately in Millie's mind. Was it there to keep people out or in?

Two young women, one a pudgy blond and the other olive-skinned with dark hair, had come out on a break to enjoy the blooming flowers. They both were wearing business suits and sat, absorbed in conversation, on a bench near the center of the grove. With Amie close behind, Millie walked casually over to them, hoping to overhear some of their conversation before she introduced herself.

". . . not what they should be. If Martin's projections hold through the next quarter, we should be in fair shape in our Asian markets."

"I hope morale holds up. Production in the mines is sagging. . . ." The woman's voice trailed off as she noticed Millie approaching.

"Hi, I'm Millie. This is my daughter, Amie."

The pudgy blond looked Millie over. "I'm Janice, this is Stasi."

The dark-haired woman smiled blandly. "Nice to meet you."

"Stasi, that's an interesting name," Millie said, returning the smile.

"It's short for Anastasia."

"You're one of those people from Earth, aren't you?" Janice asked, matter-of-factly.

Millie considered a lie but thought better of it. "Yes, I am. How did you know?"

"We know everyone in the building by first names. Take Stasi here, for instance. I've known her since preschool. Everyone working in the Administration Building is either someone I grew up with or the parent of someone I grew up with."

"It must seem like one big family," Millie observed.

Janice pulled the hair on the left side of her head back behind her ear. "Mmm. I suppose there's some comfort in such a tightly knit group, but it does have its drawbacks."

"Such as?"

"Well, there aren't many secrets here, for one thing."

"I should think that would be a benefit."

"Not really. All it means is that you can't get away with anything."

Millie tried to change the subject without seeming too inquisitive. "This is such a beautiful garden. Why is that ugly barbed wire on top of the walls?"

"To keep the Trabs out."

Millie raised her eyebrows. "Trabs?"

"The workers. They used to try to get in here. I don't know why. Probably to pick the flowers or something."

Stasi's eyes flashed angrily. "They're never satisfied. Why can't they just stay where they belong?"

"And where do they belong?" Millie asked.

"In the town. Or the mines. Anywhere but up here."

"Why do they frighten you, Stasi?"

"Because they're filthy little scavengers who wouldn't think twice about cutting our throats."

Janice nodded agreement, and Millie felt that, for the moment anyway, they had forgotten who she was. "The people I saw in town yesterday looked nice enough."

"Oh, you mean Sammy's Players? Sure, they all. . . ."

"Stasi! Hold your tongue!"

Stasi clamped both hands over her mouth, looking in terror from Janice to Millie. Millie felt sorry for the young woman, but she was grateful for the information. Stasi scrambled to cover up.

"Please don't tell anyone what I said. They'll cut my pay and ration my food. I might even end up hauling trash to the incinerator. Please."

"Don't worry, Stasi. I won't get you in trouble."

Janice grabbed Stasi by the wrist. "We have to go," she said hurriedly and dragged her friend back into the building. Millie turned to Amie.

"What do you think?"

"I think it wouldn't surprise me to find a sign on the wall that says, RICH PEOPLE ONLY."

Millie nodded. "We should tell your father before he makes any final negotiations."

When Brice returned to the conference room, Nathan was already becoming impatient. Brice assured him that arrangements were being made for a town meeting and asked Nathan to follow him down to the tube car loading dock. They took the elevator down to the ground floor without further ceremony, but Nathan could tell Brice was stalling for time.

He climbed into one of the tube cars, and Brice leaned inside, pressed the number 9 key, and thumbed the red button. Nathan scanned the numbered list of locations inside the three domes and saw that location 9 was inside the agricultural dome.

"Hey! Wait a minute!" he protested. But the canopy closed overhead, and the tube car shot out of the loading bay. The ride to Dome Three was exciting, but Nathan was in no mood to enjoy it. He had a minute and forty seconds to fume before his car finally came to a stop, and another twenty seconds before Brice arrived behind him.

"What is the meaning of this?" Nathan demanded, outraged.

"Calm yourself, Doctor Graham. I felt it necessary to show you the Agridome, since it is so important to our culture here on Venus."

Still unconvinced, Nathan followed Brice through the large door leading into Dome Three. As much as he hated being given the runaround, the view inside the agricultural dome was worth it. Rolling fields of green grass stretched out before him as far as the eye could see, and a mile away, herds of cattle were grazing. The fields extended up the mountainside until they met the dome. The top of the dome was equipped with a complicated array of pumping and filtration units, but the industrial appearance did not detract from the vista.

While Nathan was absorbed in the view, Brice surreptitiously slipped an oxygen mask off a rack near the door, holding it behind his back. He put a hand on Nathan's shoulder and nodded toward the cows.

"Let's take a closer look at the cows. There's something I wanted to show you."

The two men started off across the field. When they had gone a quarter-mile, Brice turned and scanned the wall of the dome until he saw two pinpoints of white. These were workers in lab coats, wearing hard hats and oxygen masks and standing on a gantry hundreds of feet up the wall. The control panels they were monitoring controlled the environmental systems of the dome.

Brice pulled the oxygen mask over his head and waved to the two workers. One of them threw a switch, and a tone sounded, sending the cattle scurrying into a nearby shelter. As Nathan watched in surprise, the shelter sealed itself, and a mechanical roar came from overhead. He looked up to see what it was, and suddenly his mouth and throat began to burn.

With increasing horror, Nathan realized the Agridome was being flooded with carbon dioxide. Clutching at his throat, he turned to Brice in panic and anger. But Brice was already running for the entrance to the dome. Up on the gantry, one of the workers realized that Nathan was in trouble and reached for the switch. His companion stopped him.

"Boss's orders."

"But he'll die."

"Yep."

The first man went for the controls anyway and was suddenly grappling for his life. The two men struggled precariously on the gantry for several moments. Suddenly the first worker managed to place his hands on the other's chest and he shoved as hard as he could. The worker stumbled backward, tumbled over the railing, and plunged screaming three hundred feet to the ground below. Scrambling, the first man punched in the emergency evacuation circuits, and the fans began turning in reverse.

Nathan was on his knees, nearly unconscious, when the oxygen began to filter down to ground level. As he struggled to stand, Brice ran up carrying an oxygen mask. Solicitously, he placed it over Nathan's head.

"I'm so sorry, Doctor Graham. I picked up a mask when I walked in out of habit, I'm afraid. When I waved at the worker up on the gantry, he must have thought I wanted a demonstration. I brought you a mask as fast as I could."

Nathan took several deep breaths. His lungs felt as if they had been scorched, and his head was pounding. "If it was an accident, why is one of the workers dead?"

"I don't know. I intend to have the matter investigated immediately. Why don't we get out of here, before anything else happens."

Brice led Nathan back across the field the way they had come in. The pumps overhead stopped their noisy chattering, another tone sounded, and the cows returned to their grazing as if nothing had happened.

Within twenty minutes of leaving the main trail, Ryan and Chris had worked their way through the woods to another part of town. Crouching in the underbrush, they peered cautiously into some poor miner's back yard. They knew it belonged to a miner because of the coal and sulfur stains on the laundry hanging on the clothesline. The house was only a mud hut with some scraggly grass for a yard, but as luck would have it, the fence in the front kept anyone on the street from seeing any activity around the house.

So far all they had seen were mud huts and shacks made from debris. Ryan was curious to know what was inside.

"What do we do now?" he hissed out of the side of his mouth.

Chris had his eyes trained on the doorway to the hut. "Now we get you some clothes."

Before Ryan could reply, his brother was up and running across the yard. He yanked a woolen robe from the clothesline and dashed back to his hiding place. To Ryan's knowledge, Chris had never stolen anything in his life. The shock of this unexpected behavior made him angry.

"What do you think you're doing?" Ryan hissed.

Chris looked annoyed. "Relax. We're just borrowing it for a while. We'll bring it back when we're done."

Borrowing something without permission seemed a lot like stealing, but Ryan was in no mood to argue the point.

"What do we need the robe for?"

"You're going to do some recon, little brother."

"Why me?"

"Because you can still pass for a kid."

Ryan opened his mouth to protest, but Chris had already headed out through the bushes. Ryan had to run to keep up. A short walk brought them to a spot where an alley came to a dead end in the woods. Before Ryan realized what was happening, Chris scooped up some dirt and smeared it on his brother's face.

"Hey!" Ryan whispered.

"Camouflage," Chris explained, with a hint of mischief in his voice.

Ryan gave his brother a nasty look. "I'll take care of it myself, thank you."

"The robe is perfect. You look like a native."

"What if someone tries to talk to me?"

"Just grunt. They'll think you're a mute. Find out what you can and meet me back here in half an hour."

Ryan looked at his brother as if to say "Who died and made you king?" but turned without another word and walked quickly down the alley. At the first intersection he looked both ways, then turned in the direction opposite from the house where Chris had pilfered the robe. He stopped again at the next cross street, relieved to find that the people he had passed had ignored him completely.

Down in the next block, Ryan spotted a market, with rows of tables stacked with various hard goods and perishables. No one took any notice of him as he mingled with the crowd, listening to any conversation he could get close enough to overhear. Most of the words were unintelligible, but occasionally someone would fire off a sentence or two in English, and Ryan would strain to catch every word.

The main topics of conversation, as near as he could tell, revolved around the generally poor quality of the merchandise and the difficulty of raising a family while working in the mines twelve hours a day. Were it not for the nervous feeling in the pit of his stomach, Ryan would have been fascinated by the various crude artifacts littering the wooden tables along the street. As it was, he had to work at keeping an interested look on his face.

Suddenly, in a flurry of motion a small table was knocked over, scattering metal trinkets and baked goods to the ground. Ryan saw a boy about his age round the corner at full speed, with two security guards close behind and gaining. There was something about his face that looked innocent, despite the suspicious circumstances, and in that instant, Ryan felt a kinship with him. Maybe it was the fact that he looked to be the same age, or maybe because he was in trouble.

Whatever the reason, as the boy passed, Ryan threw himself at the guards' legs, taking them both down. The boy stopped, hearing the commotion, and doubled back. He pulled Ryan to his feet and dragged him down a side street. Ryan recovered his balance, and they both took off running, dodging through back alleys, shacks, and yards until they came to a small mud hut near the edge of town. The boy led the way inside and then slammed the door, holding his side.

Neither could speak for a minute. Ryan looked around the room. In the dim light from the window, there wasn't much to see; the furniture consisted of a few blocks of wood and a couple of filthy mattresses. He had never seen such squalor up close and found it hard to believe that anyone could actually live this way. Ryan was embarrassed, and then immediately felt ashamed for feeling embarrassed. But the boy, taking in Ryan's dirty face and tattered clothes, took him for a comrade. He walked over to one of the beds and dropped a leather pouch on the mattress.

"Thank you. You saved my life back there."

"You're welcome. Why were they chasing you?"

"I'd rather not say." The boy held out a hand, and Ryan shook it. "I am Tristan Djirrin. Welcome to my home."

"Thank you."

"And by what name are you called?"

"I'd rather not say."

Tristan smiled. "You are welcome, anyway. Can I get you something to eat?"

"No, thanks. I had a big breakfast."

"Your father works in the Agridome?"

Ryan realized he had to choose his words carefully. "Uh, no. What does your dad do?"

"He's dead. Killed in a cave-in years ago. My mother works at the washer's well."

"The washer's well?"

Tristan gave him a strange look, and it occurred to Ryan that the washer's well was probably a place so well known to the townspeople, that only an outsider would ask such a question. Before he had a chance to answer, the front door opened. A middle-aged woman with dark hair and a kind, though somewhat rugged, face came through the doorway with a load of laundry.

"I see we have a visitor. Tris, please help your poor mother. Some of these clothes need mending."

"Mother, they don't even pay you. Why do you do it?"

Tristan's mother smiled serenely. "It pleases the Master." She set the load down and looked Ryan over top to bottom. "Now, who have we here?"

Tristan interceded quickly, not wishing to offend his guest. "He's a friend. He prefers to not reveal his name."

His mother eyed Ryan closely, then walked over to him, peering into his face. "You have a fair complexion. No mine worker, this one." She grabbed one of Ryan's hands and examined it. "No worker at all, by the look of his hands. Who are you, boy?"

"Please, Mother! He saved my life today."

"And what were you doing that you needed saving? Stealing for the Brotherhood, I suppose."

"Mother!"

Mrs. Djirrin acknowledged the slip by pursing her lips together tightly. Tristan stepped closer to Ryan, trying to discern by his face whether he understood what was said.

Ryan suddenly felt very uncomfortable. "Look, I have no idea what you're talking about. My name is Ryan Graham, and I'm just. . . ."

Mrs. Djirrin's eyes widened and she took several steps back. "Graham? Graham, did'ja say? You? The Destroyer?"

"Certainly not, Mother! 'Tis coincidence only!"

"Coincidence or no, he must leave us at once. It would do no good for the guards to find him here."

Tristan started to protest, but Ryan cut him off. "No, she's right. I have to go."

Tristan walked him to the door and pointed down the street. "Turn left on that road, then take your next right. You will be on a main street, which goes most of the way through town."

"Thanks. Try and stay out of trouble." Ryan smiled and left, glancing around nervously to see if he was being watched.

He reached the main thoroughfare and stopped, unsure of what to do next. As he stood on the corner trying to choose a direction, a horn sounded in the center of town. The effect on the townspeople was dramatic. They stopped immediately their activity and started walking toward the center of town. Not wishing to be discovered, Ryan decided to mingle with the crowd.

Five minutes later, he found himself in a large square in the center of town. The open area was rapidly filling with people from all directions. From a large, gnarled black tree in the center hung a dead man by a rope.

Listening to the people around him, he discovered that some were speaking passable English and decided to take a chance. He moved closer to an elderly woman at the edge of the crowd and pointed at the body.

"What happened to him?"

The woman eyed him strangely, and for a moment Ryan thought he was in trouble.

"Where were you yesterday?" the woman asked rhetorically. "Drunk or in the mines, I'll wager. He's a thief, and if you ask me, he got off too easy."

Ryan suddenly became acutely aware of the stolen robe he was wearing. A similar fate might befall him if he weren't more careful. He moved quietly away from the old woman, deciding he had better keep his mouth shut, and stood at the edge of the crowd to see what would happen next. He didn't have to wait long.

Three men in business suits ascended a platform that stood before the tree, their fine appearance a sharp contrast to the shabby peasants of the crowd. With considerable shock Ryan realized that the three men were his father, Brice Maddock, and Sammy Vile. Brice raised his arms and the crowd fell into hushed silence.

"Friends and neighbors! I bring before you today a man from Earth, who wishes to be heard by you."

Brice stepped aside and looked at Nathan. It was a strange introduction, but Nathan took the platform confidently.

"Good morning, ladies and gentlemen. My name is Doctor Nathan Graham, and I am a representative of. . . ."

His introductory remarks were cut short by a horrifying scream from the far side of the crowd. Ryan craned his neck to see and was just able to make out an old hag with her head back and mouth wide open.

"Deeestroyyyer! Deeestroyyyer!"

The crowd began to ripple with murmuring.

"It's him!"

"The prophecy! The prophecy!"

The murmur quickly grew to a roar, and the people nearest

the platform strained forward to grab hold of Nathan. An ugly mob scene was imminent and a squad of security guards with laser rifles swarmed the platform, hustling Brice, Sammy, and Nathan through the crowd and into the relative safety of the Detention Center on the far side of the square. The roar of the crowd gradually fell into a chant, and it took Ryan several seconds to decipher what they were saying.

"Ju–das! Ju–das! *Ju–das!*"

Brice reemerged from the Detention Center and mounted a fifty gallon drum near the door. Ryan was worried for fear the crowd would attack, but he raised his arms again and the crowd grew quiet.

"Cursed is he who hangs on a tree!" Brice yelled.

The crowd cheered, and sporadic chants of "Ju–das!" broke out from various portions of the square. Brice held up his hand and continued.

"Tomorrow morning, by the will of the people, the one who is called by the name of Graham, and all of his conspirators from Earth, shall hang like this thief from the Judas tree!"

The crowd cheered again, and the chanting resumed. Ryan's mouth hung open in shock, and fear clutched at his chest. Barely able to believe what he had just heard, he edged his way out of the crowd. When he reached the street, he turned and kicked into high gear. Retracing his steps, he found the deserted alley and dove into the scraggly bushes at the end of the short street. Astonished by his brother's agitated state, Chris stepped from his hiding place and scanned the alley for pursuers. The road was deserted. He grabbed Ryan by the shoulders and shook him, hard.

"What happened?"

"They got Dad!"

"What do you mean, *They got Dad?* He's in a meeting at the Administration Building."

Ryan shook his head in anguish. "No! He came down to talk to the townspeople for some reason. As soon as he introduced himself, they called him Judas and threw him in jail. Brice Maddock is planning to kill us!"

Chris looked grim. "I gotta warn Mom and Amie."

"I'll come with you."

"Hold it. I did a little recon myself while you were gone. Five hundred feet farther on there's a tube car loading station. Try to get back to the ore ship in the launching structure. We'll try to meet you there. Whether we make it or not, look for Captain Fairborne and send a message to Earth."

Ryan ran a hand through his hair and noticed he was still wearing the robe. He shuddered and tore the garment from his body, wadding it up and throwing it hard at his brother's chest.

"Hey, take it easy!" Chris said.

"They hang thieves here," Ryan replied acidly.

Chris looked down at the fabric in his hands and felt sick. "I didn't know."

Ryan's eyes softened. "Neither did I."

They prayed earnestly for God's protection, then Chris mussed Ryan's hair and told him to take care. The two brothers headed off through the woods in opposite directions. Chris was careful to drape the robe back over the clothesline of its rightful owner.

After their detour through the park, Millie and Amie had searched the first four floors of the Administration Building, noting points of interest—such as the communications center— and were starting to explore the fifth floor. Millie thought she had a pretty good feel for the layout of the building, and Amie was making a mental list of the facilities they had encountered.

At the end of a long hall, they rounded a corner and came face to face with four security guards holding laser rifles. One stepped forward.

"End of the line, ladies. Come with us, please."

When Chris reached the top of the hill, he skirted the Administration Building and found a side entrance. The door appeared to be unguarded, so he slipped inside and made his way back to their room.

He was standing in front of the door to the suite before he

remembered that he didn't have a key. He thumbed the call button on the control panel, and the door opened, revealing two security guards with their weapons drawn.

"Step inside, please. Carefully."

For just an instant Chris had the impulse to run, but in a heartbeat he remembered the conversations he had had with his father about the statistical likelihood of dodging a laser beam. He stepped through the doorway and stood very, very still.

Ryan ran as fast as he could through the woods, until at last he saw the loading dock, right where Chris said it would be. There were plenty of tube cars, but the dock was deserted, as the townspeople were still gathered in the square for the meeting.

Terror clouded his mind, making it difficult to think. Five simple words burst in upon his mind, and he began saying them over and over to himself.

"Perfect love casts out fear. Perfect love casts out fear. . . ."

Much to his relief, the terror began to subside, and he was able to move again. He ran across the dock and climbed into the nearest tube car, punching in the number for the launch bay and hitting the green button. The canopy closed overhead, and the tube car slid onto the main track as before, and Ryan was whisked on his way.

Feeling safe for the moment, Ryan began plotting what he would do once he was aboard the ore ship. If he remembered correctly, the command module was just forward of the side entryway. With a little luck, he could sneak on board and fire a message off to Earth before anyone even knew he was on board.

Ryan's car coasted into the loading area adjacent to the launch bay, and through the canopy he saw two security guards on either side of the door into the bay. Remembering something he had once read in a missionary newsletter, he closed his eyes and offered up a desperate prayer.

"Lord, as You made blind eyes see, make seeing eyes blind."

The car came to a stop and the canopy opened. The guards stared right at him as he climbed out and started toward the door. They began walking toward him, but he looked straight ahead and kept walking with grim determination. The guards brushed past him on either side, stopping when they reached the car.

The first guard looked inside the passenger compartment. "It's empty."

"That's odd. Why send a car downline without anyone in it?"

The entry doors slid open and Ryan walked through without looking back. The guards continued peering into the car in confusion. As the doors closed behind him, Ryan felt a surge of elation at God's answer to his prayer, but the exuberance left him quickly when he saw the crew of the freighter still loading containers into the cargo hold.

Not knowing whom to trust, he thought it best to wait until the foot traffic lightened up a bit before trying to get into the ship. He crept along the edge of the launch bay until he came to a pile of shipping containers. Squeezing into a small space in the shadows, with a clear view of the loading operation, he settled in for a long wait.

CHAPTER 3

The jail cell was clean and fairly modern for a remote colony, but Nathan was still shell-shocked by the recent turn events had taken. He had just begun to pray for the safety of his family, when Millie and Amie were brought into the cell block and herded into his cell. As soon as the guard left, Nathan spoke in a hushed whisper.

"Are you two all right?"

Millie nodded. "We're fine."

"Any sign of the boys?"

"No. Nathan, what happened?"

"I don't know. Something strange is going on here. Brice made a power play during the negotiations, so I called his hand and asked for a town meeting. But when I introduced myself to the people, the name *Graham* almost started a riot. They threw me in jail, and now here you are."

"At least Chris and Ryan are still free."

A few minutes later, Chris was brought in. His family gathered around him as the guards clanged the door to the cell block shut ominously.

"Are you all right? Where's Ryan?" Nathan asked.

"I'm fine. I sent him to the ore ship to radio for help."

"By himself?"

"I had to try and warn Mom and Amie." He smiled apologetically. "Sorry I wasn't fast enough."

Nathan continued. "Then you saw what happened?"

"Ryan did. He said you were thrown in jail and that Brice Maddock was going to have us killed."

Amie turned white. "But why?"

Nathan looked speculatively toward the door. "I suspect we're interfering with his plans. I am so sorry. I thought this would be business as usual. Apparently, God is using a different game plan."

"Then we'd better start using the same one," Millie said solemnly.

The Grahams knelt together in the middle of the cell and began to pray.

Hidden among the shipping containers in the launch bay, Ryan had fallen asleep. When he awoke with a start several hours later, the flurry of activity around the ore ship had dwindled to almost nothing. Over the next hour, the loading crews finished up and trudged up the ramp into the ship. Then all was quiet.

Ryan waited several minutes to make sure the area was truly deserted, and then made his way around the edge of the bay toward the ship. A walk of nearly a quarter-mile brought him to the back where the main thrusters were, and he stopped for a moment, imagining what it would be like to be standing behind the ship when the engines were at full thrust.

The ramp was several hundred feet away, at the front of the ship, which meant he was going to be out in the open for this last bit. He walked the length of the ship, trying to keep to the shadows, and was almost to the ramp when a shadow came away from one of the landing struts. A pair of rough hands spun him around and clamped his mouth shut.

It was Garushta Fairborne. Ryan's eyes widened and he cried out, the sound muffled by the captain's hand.

"Captain!"

"Shh!" Fairborne pressed his mouth close to Ryan's ear. "Go inside you must not. Guards are waiting."

He signaled for Ryan to follow him. They walked back along the ship, continuing around the edge of the launch bay until they reached the back side behind the ship. The captain stopped beside a large air compressor bolted to the floor, looked around to make sure they were alone, then got down on his hands and knees.

Ryan watched with growing curiosity as the captain unscrewed three of the bolts with his bare hands and slid the compressor to one side. The hole beneath was large enough for a man to climb down, and Ryan could see the top of a ladder.

The captain looked around nervously. "Down you must go, and not come back."

Ryan hesitated, but he knew he was out of options.

"Soonest!" the captain whispered.

Ryan nodded his thanks and climbed in, pausing just inside the hole. Then the air compressor was bolted back into place overhead, and it was pitch black. Ryan continued down the ladder, feeling his way along, hoping there would be light somewhere below. He hit bottom after thirty seconds or so and gave up any hope of finding illumination.

It was difficult to judge distance in the dark, but he guessed he had gone down about thirty feet. With his arms stretched out in front of him, he pressed his back against the ladder and started walking. He hit the opposite wall after three steps.

Panic gripped him for an instant. The narrow width of the place meant he was either in a small chamber—would it be his tomb?—or a passageway. He was willing to bet that Captain Fairborne would not bury him alive, but he still asked the Lord to please let it be a passage.

Facing the wall opposite the ladder, he guessed the entry to the launch bay to be behind him. That meant if he turned to the right down the passage, he should be headed in the general direction of the dome where his family was. There was only one way to find out.

Placing his left hand on the wall and groping in the air with his right, Ryan started blindly down the passage.

Brice Maddock sat in his office, basking in the glow of his own brilliance. His plans had taken an unusual twist, but the new plan looked to have better possibilities than the original. Sammy Vile's men who caused the cave-in off shaft number six had done their work well, for it was mid-afternoon before Halton Maddock stormed into his son's office.

"Will you please tell me what is going on?" Halton demanded, placing his hands squarely on the desk and leaning forward angrily.

Brice stood up immediately and put on a perplexed expression designed to placate his father. "You're not going to believe it, Dad. We continued with the meeting after you left, but Doctor Graham began deviating from the written proposal. He tried to cut the benefits to the townspeople and make a straight business arrangement with the company. I told him I couldn't authorize that without consulting the people. He insisted on doing it immediately, or the deal was off."

Halton was pacing. "But how did he end up in the Detention Center?"

"When I presented his case, the crowd got ugly pretty fast. I had to lock him up just to save his life."

"What about his family?"

"They're safe in their suite, under guard."

Halton shook his head in frustration. "That fool! I thought Nathan was smarter than that. It will take us a week just to calm everyone down. Will we be able to get the next shipment out on schedule?"

"No problem. I have people at work minimizing the damage even as we speak."

Halton stopped his nervous walking up and down and smiled approvingly. "Good boy. I knew you'd do the right thing. Keep me posted."

"Will do," Brice replied, returning the smile. Halton patted him on the shoulder, turned, and walked out. The smile left Brice's face immediately. He sat back down at his desk and called Sammy Vile's residence, a plush apartment on the top floor of the Administration Building. When the attempt produced no answer, he called the security station on the ground floor.

"Is Sammy Vile in the building?"

"He never returned from town, sir."

Brice closed the connection. *That's strange,* he thought, *I gave him direct orders to come back here and await my instructions. He's probably out drinking.* Brice leaned back in his chair and pulled a private list of call numbers out of his pocket. Keying in the number, he only had to wait a few moments for the party on the other end to pick up.

"Lormock."

"Mr. Lormock? This is Brice. I have some more work for you."

"No! Please, Mr. Maddock, you said the job six months ago would be the last."

"I am in no mood to argue, Mr. Lormock. Unless, of course, you want the families of your victims to hear about your handiwork."

The voice on the other end was silent for a moment, then asked tonelessly, "What is it?"

Brice leaned back in his chair, a thin smile playing at his lips. "I want you to perform a little maintenance on my father's emergency tube car. You will rewire it so that when he uses it, the failsafe will be disabled and the purge circuits engaged."

"But if I do that, your father will be blown out of the dome and . . ."

Brice finished for him. ". . . and dashed to pieces on the rocks outside. Yes, I know. Just do it."

He terminated the connection, stood and stretched, and gazed out the window without a hint of remorse.

"This day just keeps getting better and better."

Slowly, steadily, Ryan continued to work his way along the passageway in the dark. He suspected he had been wandering for well over an hour, but he had given up trying to keep track of time. The going was slow. He feared falling down an unseen hole, and the passage seemed to go on and on without end.

When the wall suddenly stopped—leaving Ryan several feet out in an open space—he was taken by surprise. Arms outstretched, he was relieved to quickly encounter another wall. Apparently, he was in a new passage running crosswise to the old one.

Ryan turned to the left, supposing it to be the way toward town, and continued through the pitch darkness. He had only gone thirty feet or so, when a light came on, blinding him, and several pairs of hands grabbed him at once. He had a brief image of four hooded figures before squeezing his eyes shut against the blinding brightness of the light.

"By what name are you called?" asked a man's voice.

"I'm Ryan Graham," Ryan said, still unable to open his eyes.

"You are part of the family from Earth?"

"Yes."

The voice chuckled and addressed the others in the group. "Bring him."

He felt the heat of the light abate and cautiously opened his eyes. He was surrounded by robed figures, two in front and two behind. The light was now shining ahead, revealing a maze of twisting passages. With a sigh of relief, Ryan decided he was glad to have been captured. He could easily have starved before finding a way out of this underground labyrinth.

They walked on for some time, turning here and there, until Ryan hardly knew which way was up. At last they emerged into a vaulted chamber some fifty feet across and roughly circular. In the center of the room stood a stone table, where five more hooded figures were seated. Their faces were obscured by the shadows.

The four guards presented Ryan and then stood at attention, ready for the slightest command. After an uncomfortable pause, the figure seated at the middle of the table spoke. His accent seemed to be a cross between German and Irish.

"By what name is he called?"

"He is Ryan Graham, of the family from Earth," the guard on Ryan's right replied.

"Ryan Graham, how did you come to be here?"

Ryan swallowed hard and decided a straight answer was the

best course. "Captain Fairborne let me in through a secret passage in the launch bay."

The figure laughed. "Good, Garushta. Gamaliel, have a calf slaughtered and delivered to Garushta's family."

"Yes, Little Poppa," said the figure seated to his left, scribbling on a piece of paper. Little Poppa continued.

"Ryan Graham, we mean you no harm. We are pleased that you have escaped your fate with the company, but your being here presents us with some difficulty. Our assembly is not generally known, and if the wrong people found out, the company would hunt us down and destroy us."

Ryan took a deep breath. "May I speak?"

"You obviously have a tongue. Use it."

"Who are you?"

"We are the Brotherhood of the Cross, the spiritual descendants of the Seer Josiah, and the servants of the Laird Jaysoos."

For a moment Ryan could not believe his ears. "Do you mean the Lord Jesus? The Messiah?"

A hush fell over the group, and when the leader, the one called Little Poppa, spoke again, his voice was edged with disbelief.

"You know of the Messiah?"

Ryan broke into a relieved grin. "I love Him! He's my Lord!"

"You serve Him?"

"My whole family does."

The leader turned to the one seated on his right. "It is as you foresaw, Elish. They are servants of the Most High." He turned his attention back to the prisoner. "Ryan Graham, we see now that your family stands wrongly accused. We are prepared to do anything within our power to prevent their deaths. Would you join with us?"

Ryan was taken aback by the turn of events, but the Brotherhood looked like the only hope for his family. With some effort, he put his misgivings aside.

"Yes, I would."

The leader turned to his scribe, Gamaliel, who also served as priest. "My friend, your services are required."

Gamaliel stood and walked to Ryan's side, producing a long

knife. The hilt was beautiful, but the blade looked razor sharp. Ryan couldn't help wondering what kind of service was required.

The priest cut Ryan's sleeve at the shoulder and tore it off, then placed the point of the blade against the skin of his upper arm. Ryan realized what was coming next. *Okay,* he thought, *so they're definitely not conservative Christians.* His instinct was to pull away, but he was loathe to offend this odd people who had offered their help. He closed his eyes and tensed every muscle in his body, waiting.

Gamaliel bowed his head for a moment. "By His stripes we are healed."

"By His stripes we are healed," the group responded.

The priest made a vertical cut and then a horizontal one in the flesh of Ryan's arm. Ryan clenched his teeth but did not cry out. The rest of the group let out a muffled cheer and threw their hoods back. The leader jumped to his feet and ran around the table, giving Ryan a bear hug. The sting from the fresh wounds made Ryan wince, and he pulled back gently, politely protesting, "I'm bleeding on your robe."

The leader stood back a step and looked at Ryan with a delighted smile on his face. "Welcome to our family, Ryan Graham. I am Klaus Darmon, but you can call me *Little Poppa*."

Klaus stood only five feet six inches, with sandy brown hair and a handsome, rugged face. He appeared to be in his early thirties, but it was hard to tell his age in the dim light.

Ryan returned the smile. "Pleased to meet you. Why do they call you *Little Poppa*? Do you have a lot of children?"

"I'm not even married," Klaus' grin broadened, "but I'm good with explosives."

Ryan was baffled. "Little Poppa? Oh! *Popper!*"

Klaus nodded, then shook his head. "You have a peculiar accent, Ryan Graham. But I dare say you might say the same about us." He turned to one of the men—a young man—seated at the end of the table, who turned out to be a familiar face. "Tristan, be a good lad and see to his shoulder, and get him some real clothes."

"Yes, Little Poppa."

"But hurry back! We have much planning to do."

The room off the passageway was small, with a single bed hewn out of the rock wall, but the bedding was thick and provided more than enough padding. Ryan sat with his feet apart, his torso turned so his wounded shoulder was easy to reach. Tristan dabbed a cloth in a wooden bowl containing some orange solution and swabbed the medication on the wound. Ryan squeezed his eyes shut and bit his lip, but he didn't pull away.

"Talk to me. It'll help me not think about the pain."

"What shall I say?"

"I don't care. Tell me about yourself. Talk about your family, the Brotherhood, anything to take my mind off what you're doing."

"I am Tristan Djirrin, son of Vanth Shawkirk Djirrin and Theresa VanHuen Djirrin. I have seen twenty-three seasons of the sun . . ."

"What is a season of the sun?"

"Venus travels around the sun. One revolution is the same as one season."

"You're twenty-three years old? No way."

"You forget we are closer to the sun."

"Oh, right. My dad told me your years are two hundred fifty-five Earth days long."

Tristan began wrapping a bandage around Ryan's arm. "Yes. I have worked in the mines since my fifteenth season."

"Your father let you work in the mines that young?"

"My father died when I was in my third season. I work in the mines to feed my family. Mother sells salves and potions to help the sick."

"I'm sorry. You told me your father was dead. Sounds like a rough life."

"We have clothes on our backs and food to eat. The Lord is good."

Ryan had to agree with that. "The Lord is good."

"The only thing I regret is having to spend so much time away from my mother. The hours in the mines are long."

"I don't suppose you can carry around a photograph."

"We are a poor people, Ryan Graham. We have no image recorders of any kind. But I do have something I carry with me." Tristan reached behind his neck and pulled a leather cord out of the opening at the top of his robe. At the end of the cord was a small ceramic bird. "This belonged to the mother of my mother's mother. My mother gave it to me, so I would never forget her."

Tristan finished tying off the bandage and handed Ryan a stack of clothes, consisting of some cloth pants, a white shirt, and a robe.

"What is Earth like, Ryan Graham?"

"A lot like your biodomes, only there's blue sky overhead and birds in the trees."

"I have learned about birds. They have wings and feathers and they fly, don't they?"

"Yes. They also eat worms and small rodents, and make a mess of your ground car if you happen to be in the wrong place at the wrong time. But most importantly, they sing."

"You mean songs?"

"Not exactly. They whistle and chirp, but they often use the same pattern and it sounds like singing."

"I would like to hear that some day."

Ryan tied his robe and faced Tristan, arms out. "How do I look?"

"Like one of us."

"Good. Tell me the truth, Tristan. Can the Brotherhood really save my family?"

"We are your only hope."

To an Earth native like Ryan, walking the streets of town in the middle of the Venusian night—in broad daylight—was an unsettling experience. Someone from the Arctic Circle would have had an easier time of it, but to Klaus Darmon, born and raised on Venus, it was perfectly natural. The biggest adjustment for him was going from the darkness underground to the light above.

Followed by two of the brethren, Klaus emerged from an abandoned building. The three hooded figures walked down the deserted street as if it were the most natural scenario to be strolling along at four in the morning. The last uprising by disgruntled townspeople had been decades ago, and the threat of the Judas tree continued to be a serious deterrent to crime, so little security was needed around town.

Unfortunately, Klaus had a job to do and a very specific place in which to do it, and there was a security guard posted within fifty feet of his target. The three men headed for the weary guard, who raised his laser rifle at their approach.

"That's far enough. What do you want?"

Klaus held his hands up in supplication. "We have business to transact."

The guard was too tired to care much. "It's a little early isn't it?"

"We require some privacy."

At this minor revelation, the guard looked around to be certain no one else was in the area.

"Privacy is a precious commodity around here."

Klaus was silent for a moment, considering his options. "And what is the going rate for privacy these days?"

"Well, if I leave my post, they dock me a week's pay, and I'm on report. For a first offense, I'd probably be back on the duty roster in two weeks."

"That doesn't sound so bad."

"My reputation means a lot to me."

Klaus reached into his robe, removed a small pouch, and handed it to the guard. The man opened it to find a dozen rare gems, though the gray light from the dome did little to show off the specular highlights of the stones.

"How much are these worth?"

"Let's just say, you could buy your own ship—maybe two."

"Reputation isn't everything. I'm going for a walk."

The guard turned and walked up an adjacent alley until he was out of sight. Klaus turned to his companions.

"Go below. There's no reason to risk three of us."

The other two men promptly walked back to the abandoned building without questioning. Klaus turned off the street to a narrow, trashy alley running parallel to the main square in the center of town. All of the shops along this particular lane had long been abandoned, and abandoned buildings were required for the kind of work he had to do.

Klaus slipped easily through the rear door of one of the smaller shops on the right hand side of the street, facing the square. Pulling a small pry bar off his belt, he knelt down and lifted one of the floorboards aside. Then he pulled what appeared to be a wad of reddish clay out of his pack and inserted a small, black box into the mass. The detonator could be triggered by remote control from up to a mile away.

He placed the explosive under the floor and replaced the board, careful to cover his tracks in the dust and grime as he left the room. The building next door was identical in layout. Klaus repeated the procedure, removing the floorboard, priming the charge, and placing it beneath the floor. Anything less than a deliberate search would reveal nothing of his activities in either building.

His task complete, Klaus started down the street to make his escape. There, up ahead stood four security guards at the intersection, rifles in hand, obviously searching the area for someone.

Klaus looked behind him. There was no escape that way, and the nearest door was fifty feet away. He turned to the side and discovered a pile of molding trash. Breathing through his mouth, he began filling his robe with the worst of the debris, promising himself a long bath later if he got out of this alive.

He happened upon two eggplants, soft with decay but not entirely rotten, and had an idea. He had just cradled the rancid vegetables in his arm when a heavy hand clamped down on his shoulder from behind.

"Did you see what happened to the guard that was stationed

here? He didn't report in on time." Klaus was surrounded by the four guards.

Klaus feigned deep thought. "Left a few minutes ago, he did. Said he had to answer the call of nature."

"What are you doing here?" one of the guards demanded.

Klaus showed his teeth and hissed as he spoke. "I am Kevas Trillium, seller of eggplants."

"I don't remember seeing any eggplant vendor before."

Klaus showed his teeth again and bowed in a self-deprecating manner. "Ay, 'tis a matter of supply. Today, the supplier gave me these." He held out the moldy eggplants, licking his lips as if they were a delicacy. "They're for sale, if you want them."

The stench from the garbage and the suggestion of eating something so hideous was intolerable. With one accord, the guards pushed Klaus toward the end of the street.

"Off with you! And take a bath, you putrid street rat!"

Klaus hobbled around the corner, calling over his shoulder as he disappeared.

"That I will do, I promise you!"

Nathan awoke early the next morning after a fitful night's sleep. The light in the jail never changed, and were it not for his chronometer, he would have had no idea what time of day it was. His dreams had been unpleasant, and the stark reality of the cold jail cell offered no comfort.

The rest of his family seemed to be resting more or less comfortably. Nathan found an open space on one of the benches along the walls and sat down. They had prayed well into the previous evening, but he was feeling a little numb in spirit. He gazed at his wife and two children and realized that it was Ryan he was most concerned about. It was hard to believe God would let them die like this, but Ryan might be dead already. Nathan pushed the thoughts from his mind and closed his eyes.

He was awakened sometime later by the clang of the cell block door sliding open. The security chief stood in the doorway.

"Morning, all! Nice day for a hanging, isn't it?"

Nathan was livid, but his voice remained steady. "We demand a fair trial by an impartial judge."

The chief laughed. "You'll get a fair trial all right—by Judge Rope and his bailiff Mr. Noose."

None of the cell guards joined in his laughter, and the chief changed his manner brusquely.

"Come on, then," he ordered sullenly. "Out with you."

The Grahams rose to their feet, looked at each other helplessly, and filed out of the cell—first Nathan, then Amie, Millie, and Chris. Four armed guards escorted them outside to the square. It was jammed with people, like the day before, but this time four ropes with nooses were hanging from the bottom branch of the Judas tree, as Brice had called it. Several people were standing on the platform below, including the security chief and Brice himself. When the crowd saw the Grahams, the people cheered like spectators at a sporting event, then took up the now-familiar chant.

"Ju–das! Ju–das!"

The Grahams were only a short distance from the platform when two explosions rocked the square. A pair of small buildings on the far side went up in twin crimson fireballs. In the smoke and confusion, a legion of hooded figures appeared from nowhere and surrounded the Grahams. The guards were disarmed and overpowered without getting off a shot, even as Brice and the security chief shouted orders over the noise of the crowd. Within seconds the hooded figures had dragged each member of the Graham family off through the crowd in different directions.

Pulled along, stumbling through the crowd, Nathan was looking back for his family. Rough hands on either side jerked him around, and a gruff voice growled in his ear, "Yer family is being taken care of, and unless you want to be killed, you'd best look out for yerself."

His escorts pressed on through the mass of bodies, roughly elbowing people out of the way, and suddenly they were through. Nathan found himself at the entrance to a narrow alley which ran up a hillside between two rows of shacks, toward the woods at the top of the hill.

The figure on his left grabbed his arm and pointed up the hill.

"Run straight up the hill. When you reach the top, ignore the warning signs and head straight into the woods."

As if to punctuate his instructions, a blast of laser fire tore over their heads and blew a hole in one of the shacks. The two hooded figures split and dashed off in opposite directions, and like a sprinter out of the starting blocks, Nathan took off up the hill, with three guards in hot pursuit.

Adrenalin coursed through his veins as he charged up the hill, and he felt almost as if he were flying. He reached the top with his thighs burning, as another laser blast grazed past him. There were signs posted everywhere: DANGER! UNMARKED MINE SHAFTS. He forced his legs to keep on moving.

The guards could see he was nearing the woods and stopped to take careful aim. Their sights were trained clearly on the center of Nathan's back, but before one guard could pull the trigger, Nathan dropped out of sight. They heard a brief cry, then silence.

Climbing to where Nathan had disappeared, the three guards saw immediately what had happened. Some rotten boards over a mine shaft had been covered by a thin layer of dirt. One of the guards picked up a large rock and dropped it down the shaft, carefully avoiding the splintered wood around the edges. The sound of the rock bouncing off the walls continued for some time, but they never heard it hit bottom.

The first guard shook his head. "Better this than the tree, I suppose."

The others nodded, and as one man they turned and headed down the hill toward the square.

Fifteen feet below the ground, just inside a passage leading away from the mine shaft, stood four hooded figures in the darkness, hovering over Nathan Graham, still tangled in the net that had saved his life.

When the explosions went off, Amie clapped her hands over her ears, even as a burly fellow in a robe picked her up and threw her over his shoulder like a sack of potatoes. Two other robed men opened a path through the crowd, and the burly one ran like a juggernaut for daylight.

Bursting through the perimeter of the crowd, he sent several townspeople sprawling, and then pounded down a side street amidst a hail of laser fire. He rounded one corner, then another, and they were at the tube car loading dock. Before Amie could say a word, he stuffed her into a car and pushed the button for the Agridome.

The car took off, and the burly man leapt over the tracks and dived into the underbrush. The security squad, hot in pursuit, arrived in time to see the car disappear into the tube. The squad leader pulled a communicator from his belt and called ahead.

Amie's tube car hurtled on through a mountainside. Suddenly in the dim light she saw another car sitting ahead in the middle of the tracks. Her heart in her mouth, she realized in a split second that there were people standing around it, and one man had a rod thrust down into the tracks.

As she raced onward, the man lifted the rod and the car in front sped away. Then immediately he jammed the rod back down into the tracks, and Amie's car came to a screeching halt. The trauma of deceleration knocked her unconscious, and when the canopy opened, several sets of strong hands lifted her gently from the car.

The front car rocketed out the far end of the tunnel under the watchful eye of two guards manning a hillside laser cannon emplacement. The empty car raced toward the edge of the dome, the gunner squeezed the trigger, and the car exploded.

The gunner pulled his communicator off his belt.

"Target destroyed. Notify maintenance we have a breach in track twelve, sector zero one four."

No sooner had Millie been pulled into the crowd than she was covered with a canvas sack and carried off. The two men carrying her were having a hard time of it, however, as the crowd was especially close to that side. A warning blast from a laser

59

rifle sent people scurrying for cover, and the two figures cut left up a broad street. Six other robed figures rolled a heavy cart into the street behind them and overturned it, blocking the view from the square.

A half dozen laser blasts hit the cart and it caught fire, but the framework held together and the smoke made visibility worse. A few moments later, six guards surrounded the burning cart only to see a horse-drawn cart full of hay speeding away fifty yards up the street, with a canvas sack on top. The guards took aim and fired, and the hay burst into flames. A woman's scream echoed down the street, as the canvas bag was engulfed by the fire.

The guards turned away, as thick clouds of greasy black smoke rose from the pyre of burning hay. Thoroughly disgusted but not wishing to admit it, the guards returned to the square to make their report to the chief.

Had they stopped for a minute to watch, they would have noticed a pile of trash come to life halfway up the street. Three figures—two men and a woman—crept stealthily into a nearby alley.

Chris was surprised by the explosions, but he knew a rescue when he saw one. Two hooded figures cleared the way, and a firm push from behind got his legs moving. Several figures formed a wedge and Chris ran behind them as they cut a path through the crowd. They reached the edge of the crowd near the end of a street.

"Straight on to the end, then right!" said a voice on his right.

"Run like a snake!" said another.

Chris thought the second command odd but ran for all he was worth. A laser blast narrowly missed his right shoulder, and then he understood. He dodged to one side and then the other, running in a serpentine pattern.

Laser fire followed him up the alley, but as the guards pursuing him were running also, the shots were not accurate. He rounded the corner at the end of the street and pulled up short. On the ground in front of him was a dead calf, and thirty feet beyond that was a uniformed guard holding a rocket launcher. He barely had time to take in the scene, when three pairs of hands grabbed him from behind.

Chris started to struggle but quickly realized the hands weren't trying to hurt him. They tore off his shirt and shoes, threw them on the carcass, and dragged him down through a hole in the ground. The last man down pulled closed a hatch camouflaged with a shallow pile of leaves.

The guard with the rocket launcher targeted the carcass and pulled the trigger. A few seconds later, three guards rounded the corner and stopped. The ground before them was strewn with the remains of the calf and bits of clothing. Nearby, one of Chris's shoes lay smoldering. Unnerved, the three guards looked a bit queasily at their comrade, but only one of them managed to say anything.

"Nice shot."

CHAPTER 4

In a passage underground, Chris was fitted with a blindfold by one of his escorts, covered with a robe, and shod with a pair of canvas shoes. The group headed off at a brisk pace, with one man on either side of Chris to help him along. At first, Chris tried to keep track of the turns in case he needed to make a quick exit, but he soon gave up as the maze proved very intricate.

After twenty minutes or so, he was led through an oak door into a chamber, and his blindfold was removed. The three hooded figures left the room, locking the door behind them, and Chris turned around to see where he was. Then he noticed he wasn't alone.

"Dad!"

The two embraced in a mixture of relief and exhaustion.

"Are you all right?"

Chris took a moment to check for injuries. "Just a few scratches."

"What happened to your shirt?"

"They threw it on a dead calf and dragged me down a hole." Nathan shook his head. "Weird."

"You're telling me. What happened to you?"

Nathan walked over to a small wooden table and poured his son a cup of water. Chris accepted it eagerly, as Nathan replied, "I fell down a mine shaft."

"It wasn't fatal, I see."

"No. Not yet, anyway."

Their conversation was interrupted as the door opened again, and Millie was brought in blindfolded. One of her escorts removed her blindfold, and a look of relief flooded her face as she recognized Nathan and Chris. Their new captors left the room and the three fell into each other's arms. After a moment, Nathan held his wife at arm's length.

"Are you okay, Millie?" he asked anxiously.

"Only bruised, I think, dear."

Nathan crinkled up his nose. "Delightful smell. What happened to you?"

"They carried me off in a canvas sack and dumped me in a pile of garbage."

"That's all?"

"No. A hay cart caught fire, and one of those fellows with the robes pulled a knife on me and told me to scream. So I did. Then they blindfolded me and brought me here."

Chris gave his dad a questioning look. "Dad, what's going on?"

"I'm not sure, but I think . . . wait a minute. You said they threw your shirt on a dead calf. Was there anyone else there?"

"There was a guard with a rocket launcher."

Nathan shook his finger thoughtfully. "That was no guard. They must have stolen a uniform. Did he fire?"

"After they pulled me down the hole."

"That has to be it. This wasn't just a rescue. They staged our deaths."

At that moment, the door opened once more, and the unconscious form of Amie was carried in and laid gently on the floor by three robed men. Two men left immediately, but a third stayed behind. The Grahams looked at him curiously, and he pulled his hood back. It was Ryan. Then they all tried to talk at once.

"Mom! Dad!"

"Hey, little brother!"

"Ryan! Thank God you're alive."

"Are you all right? What happened to Amie?"

"Amie suffered a little deceleration trauma during her escape. The priest says she should be coming around anytime now."

Nathan looked at Amie cautiously, and then said, "Why don't we all sit down and you tell us everything you know."

The family took a moment to get situated in a rough circle on the floor, before Ryan spoke up.

"After I saw Dad thrown into jail, Chris and I decided to split up. . . ."

Ryan's story took almost a half hour, and halfway through Amie roused, much to everyone's relief. When he had finished, and filled in Amie as well, the family was silent.

"So the company thinks we're dead?" Nathan asked at last.

"I think all the teams were successful. So far as the company is concerned, I'm the only one unaccounted for, and I doubt they see me as much of a threat."

"Why are they keeping us locked up if they're Christians?" Amie asked, puzzled.

"You haven't been through the initiation ritual."

Amie grimaced. "You mean we have to have crosses cut into our arms?"

"Unless you can convince them it isn't necessary."

Amie turned to her father. "Oh, Daddy, please do. I hate the sight of blood, especially when it's mine."

Nathan smiled and patted his daughter on the leg. "Don't worry. I'll think of something."

Only moments later, a hooded figure entered the room and whispered to Ryan.

"He wants us to follow him," Ryan explained.

The Grahams walked down a short passageway and into the same meeting chamber where Ryan was initiated into the Brotherhood. Nathan was separated from his family and brought before the stone table. Ryan noticed the council seemed to have assigned seats, as everyone was in the same place as before.

The leader addressed Nathan. "Nathan Graham, your son tells us that you all serve Jesus the Messiah. Is this true?"

"It is."

"Then we pledge you our hospitality. But if you would move freely among us, you must join with us. Do you know what this means?"

"My son has explained it to me. We all wish to join you."

Gamaliel the chief priest stood and moved to Nathan's side, taking out his dagger. He removed Nathan's sleeve and placed the point of the dagger against the skin of his shoulder.

"By His stripes we are healed."

Before the others could respond, Nathan interrupted. "Wait!"

Gamaliel stepped back in shock, and a hush fell over the room.

"Please forgive me," Nathan continued. "I mean you no disrespect, but this is wrong. It goes against the Word of God."

"Explain," the leader replied.

"The priest just said, 'By His stripes we are healed.' It is *His* stripes, not ours. God said, 'I will put My law in their minds, and write it *on their hearts;* and I will be their God, and they shall be My people.'"

Gamaliel frowned. "But for one to be saved, blood must be shed."

"Don't you see? It's already been done. The sacrifice of Jesus on the cross is complete. In fact, in the Bible it is often the enemies of God who gash themselves with sharp instruments."

The leader stood up slowly. "You have read the Bible?"

"Yes, of course. Haven't you?"

"We have never seen one. Our chief priest is the keeper of the sacred words." The leader paused thoughtfully for a moment. "What you are saying is difficult for us to hear. Would you submit to a test?"

"Certainly."

Gamaliel stood up and pulled a small, tattered, spiral-bound notebook from his robe, and began to read.

"'In the beginning was the Word. . . .'" He paused as if waiting for the rest.

"'. . . and the Word was with God, and the Word was God;'" Nathan replied.

Gamaliel registered surprise, and there was a hushed murmur

from the others, but the priest turned several pages and continued.

"'Be anxious for nothing, but in everything by prayer and supplication, with thanksgiving, let your requests be made known to God . . .'"

"'. . . and the peace of God, which surpasses all understanding, will guard your hearts and minds through Christ Jesus,'" Nathan finished.

The leader held up his hand. "Enough. There is no question, you know the Word of God. If what you have said is true, we must change our rite of initiation. In the meantime, how can we trust you?"

Nathan was quiet for a moment. "We believe in the same Lord. His Word is our bond."

Now it was the leader's turn to be silent for a moment. "Well said. So be it."

The leader pulled his hood back. "I am Klaus Darmon. Welcome to our family, Nathan Graham."

Hoods slowly came down all around the room, and Nathan signaled for his family to join him.

"We appreciate very much your saving our lives, Mr. Darmon."

"Please, call me *Little Poppa*."

At the curious look on Nathan's face, Ryan responded. "He was responsible for the pyrotechnics at the square this morning. It's not *Poppa* as in *Daddy,* but *Popper* as in *Kaboom*."

Nathan smiled at Klaus. "Tastefully done. I don't think anyone was hurt. But you would do me honor, if you would allow me to call you *Klaus*."

"Very well, Nathan. But let's dispense with the pleasantries. I'm willing to bet a dozen cattle that you haven't had anything to eat since yesterday. Am I right?" The new arrivals all nodded vigorously, and Klaus continued. "Follow me, please."

A short while later, a sumptuous meal was served in another, larger room furnished with long tables and benches. On the walls were layers of shelves lined with vacuum containers of food and kegs of a cider-like beverage. At the sight of such bounty, the Grahams joined hands, and the others in the room followed suit. Nathan thanked God for the food, for His gracious deliverance, and for the hospitality of their hosts, and everyone echoed *Amen*.

When the meal was finished, after an appropriate interval Klaus held up his hand until all the conversations ebbed to silence.

"I have been thinking about your knowledge of the Bible, family from Earth, and something troubles me. I want to ask for your help, but I do not wish to be a poor host."

"We owe you our lives. Ask whatever you want," Nathan replied.

"I cannot break my oath as host by putting the burden of decision on you."

Nathan sensed that this exchange was very personal and chose his words carefully. "Is there any way to relieve you of your oath?"

Klaus smiled, pleased that Nathan understood. "As my guests, you may ask me questions."

Nathan understood. "Ryan told me you refer to yourselves as the spiritual descendants of the Seer Josiah. What exactly does that mean?"

"Catherine Josiah was the Seer for the people many years ago."

"When you say *Seer*, do you mean she was a prophetess?" Nathan asked.

"And more. Her father came to Venus as the chaplain on one of the first ships. When he was killed in a mine accident, she took his place. She got in trouble when she started trying to restore ownership of the mines to the people."

"Restore ownership?"

"In the beginning, the mines belonged to the colonists. It was one of the reasons so many signed on to come to Venus. By giving mine shares to the colonists, the company was protected. If the mines dried up, too bad for the colonists. If the mines were successful, the company still made a respectable profit. Nobody considered the possibility that the mines would make people rich beyond their wildest dreams. The company began holding back profits from the colonists. The hardships of life in the domes prevented them from discovering this robbery until it was too late."

"What kind of hardships?"

"Some of the environmental engineers had miscalculated the acidity in the atmosphere, and the carbon dioxide filters were inadequate to the task of protecting the crops. Things were bad at first with crops dying and people going hungry. The company offered to intervene, but only if the colonists sold their rights to the mines back to the company. A few brave souls tried to hold out, but it was useless. In the end, the company bought up everything, and the colonists became slave labor."

"Why didn't the colonists just pack up and go back to Earth?"

"They didn't have the resources. The company set transport prices so high, no one could afford to leave."

Nathan shook his head. "But why didn't they take over the Administration Building by force or send a message to Earth?"

"Terrence Maddock was a crafty one. He must have been planning to take over the operation from the beginning. When things got bad, he hired a security force from Earth, supposedly to keep the peace during food shortages. They became the company police force. The communications center was located inside the Administration Building, and no one was allowed inside."

"But surely, the security force would die out after one generation, or someone of conscience would get the word out," Millie interjected.

"They replace the entire security force every five years. You have to understand this is a very lucrative contract for the security company. They're not about to spoil the meat."

Millie looked sad. "It sounds like the old Iron Curtain."

Klaus was interested. "What is this *Iron Curtain?*"

"In the late twentieth century, several countries—of which the Soviet Union was the largest—were known as the Eastern bloc. These were police states, with walls around their borders to keep people inside, very much like what you have here. In these countries, all the resources were controlled by a few powerful people, who enforced their wishes through the military while the rest of the population lived in poverty."

"What happened to this Eastern bloc?"

"The people decided they had had enough and there was revolution. The walls came down."

Klaus looked thoughtful. "We could use a little revolution here."

"So, what happened to Catherine Josiah?" Chris asked.

"After conditions began to improve for the colonists, she demanded that the company give them the opportunity to buy back their shares of the mines. She went head to head with Terrence Maddock and wouldn't back down. The people began to smell victory, and even the security force began to fear for their safety. Then suddenly the negotiations stopped. Catherine Josiah turned up missing. Nobody knows for sure what happened to her—she disappeared without a trace. Some say she was shipped back to Earth, others say she was murdered. One thing we know for certain: She was betrayed."

Nathan raised his eyebrows. "You would think if they shipped her back to Earth, she would have found some way to contact the Interstellar Trade Commission."

Chris wasn't so sure. "Not necessarily. They may have threatened to kill the people she left behind if she didn't keep her mouth shut."

"Either way, she sounds like a remarkable woman. It's hard to imagine anyone betraying her."

"Aye, it is. Nevertheless, in the months before her disappearance her apprentice began privately to slander her name to the people. Catherine had taken in Lebezej Kraal as a pupil, but because of her exhaustive efforts on behalf of the people, she was not as attentive to her as she should have been. Kraal began dabbling in the black arts and acquired a taste for it. She began turning the hearts of the people against Catherine, and the believers in Christ fell under heavy persecution."

"That's why you went underground!" Ryan exclaimed, finally seeing the picture.

"Exactly. Our grandparents were children at the time, and they stayed underground for many years before finally venturing forth as adults, to live in shelters and work the mines like the rest of the people. And so we have lived for over one hundred years, half in this world, half in the world above."

"What happened to that Kraal woman?" Ryan asked.

"Immediately after Catherine's disappearance, Lebezej Kraal declared herself the new Seer and made a secret alliance with the Maddocks. This gave her great power, which no one dared to come against."

Millie chafed at the thought of justice trampled. "Then her treachery went unpunished?"

"Not exactly. Once she was firmly established, she instituted the Judas tree—I believe you've seen it—from which criminals would hang. This gave her a convenient way to dispose of her detractors."

Amie shuddered, and Klaus put a comforting hand on her shoulder before continuing.

"Lebezej Kraal gave birth to a daughter she named Saphirra, and the daughter learned her mother's ways only too well. When she was only twenty, Saphirra stole from the chief of security and denounced her mother as the thief. Saphirra watched her mother hang from the Judas tree, declaring herself the new seer that same day."

Chris grimaced. "Nice family."

"Reminds me of Haaman," Millie murmured.

"Who is Haaman?" Klaus asked, curious.

"An evil servant of an old king. He's in the book of Esther in the Bible. He built a gallows on which to hang Mordecai, one of God's servants. But through the faithful actions of Esther, another of God's servants, the tables were turned, and Haaman was hung on his own gallows."

"You say this story is from the Bible?" Klaus asked enviously.

"Yes," Millie replied, thinking of her own well-marked Bible back in her suitcase. She didn't have even a pocket Testament now to give to these people who were so hungry for God's Word.

Nathan addressed Klaus. "Is Saphirra Kraal still alive?"

"She is the Seer, the very one who denounced you before the assembly yesterday."

Millie was perplexed. "Why would she do that?"

"If she's in league with Brice Maddock, it would explain a lot," Nathan offered.

"There's more to it than that," Klaus responded. "After her mother's death, she made a pact with the powers of darkness, trading her eyes for the gift of prophecy. For many years she has foreseen your coming—that you would come from far away to destroy us all. She has foretold many things that have come to pass, so even we as Christians were not sure what to think upon your arrival."

Nathan reached for a mug of cider. "What changed your mind?"

"A week before your arrival, one of our number, a man named Elish, had a dream. In this dream, he was standing before the Word of God, and the Book spoke, saying that you were all servants of the Most High. When we questioned your son, we found out it was true."

Nathan shot a brief, *That's my boy* look in Ryan's direction. "Good work, Ryan. Your profession of faith saved our lives."

Ryan blushed but said nothing.

"Now maybe you can save our lives," Klaus said solemnly.

"What do you mean?"

"Until today, our existence has been a secret. Why the Seer has been unaware of us, I do not know. Perhaps it is the protection of God's angels. But after this morning's events, the company must know for certain that there is an underground of resistance. We have reason to believe that Brice Maddock plans to murder his father and take over the company. With Halton Maddock out of the way, they will hunt us down and kill us."

"What makes you think Brice is going to murder his father?"

"Before you were rescued, three of our number brought Sammy Vile here. He is not a brave man. It didn't take much to loosen his tongue."

"How can we help?"

Gamaliel produced a strong box from a niche in the wall of

the chamber and carried it over to the table. Klaus slid the box over in front of Nathan, inviting him to examine it.

"This was found in Catherine Josiah's quarters after her disappearance. It has been locked for more than a hundred years. The lock cannot be opened, and we have found the metal to be impervious to all of our tools. Even diamond drills will not scratch it. Perhaps it was her father's. Anyway, all attempts to open it have failed."

"Do you have any idea what happened to the key?"

Gamaliel took out a ragged piece of paper from his pocket and laid it out on the table in front of Nathan, who peered at the faded words.

"A poem?"

Klaus nodded. "It was found with the box. Read it."

Nathan held the piece of paper out a bit so he could focus more easily.

> *How lovely on the river bed,*
> *Are the hands of the handmaiden,*
> *Forming God's creature for the fiery furnace,*
> *When her good work is done,*
> *And the battle be ended,*
> *Find the key at the heart of the Spirit,*
> *descended.*

Nathan looked around the group, receiving only blank stares in return. "You don't have any idea what this means, do you?"

Gamaliel shook his head. "We have spent many long years trying to decipher its meaning."

Chris volunteered. "Let's try it step by step. What does the first part mean?"

"I don't know. Why would a handmaiden have her hands on a river bed?" Millie asked.

"Maybe she was collecting something, like water or rocks."

Nathan looked at the poem again. "No, it has to be something malleable. The next line says, 'Forming God's creature for the fiery furnace.'"

Chris nodded. "Clay, then. You get it from the river bed and fire it in a furnace."

Nathan pointed at Chris. "Right! Good. Okay, the handmaiden makes something and fires it in a furnace. But then she has to wait until 'the battle be ended.' What does that mean?"

Millie frowned. "What was Klaus just telling us? Catherine went head to head with Terrence Maddock. Sounds like a battle to me."

Excitement was building in the room, and Chris could feel it. "That's got to be it. If there's something valuable in that box, you wouldn't want to open it in the middle of a conflict. You'd wait until the battle was over. Only in this case, the battle never really ended. Catherine disappeared."

Nathan read from the paper once more. "Which brings us to the last line. 'Find the key at the heart of the Spirit, descended.' Any ideas?"

"It must be the Holy Spirit," Millie offered.

"Agreed. What do we know about the Holy Spirit?"

Chris was searching his memory. "There's the stuff at Pentecost with the tongues of fire. That might tie in somehow with the furnace. Most of the other references I can think of have to do with divine messages or people being struck dead."

"Neither of which help us very much," Nathan observed, reading the poem through again. "It says 'the Spirit, descended.' When did the Spirit descend?"

"At Pentecost," Chris repeated.

Millie gasped. "No! Not only at Pentecost. At Christ's baptism, the Spirit descended in bodily form like a dove."

"A dove! That's it! One of God's creatures formed out of clay and fired in the furnace." Nathan thumped the piece of paper on the table in front of him.

Millie was perplexed. "But who is the handmaiden?"

Klaus had an answer to that one. "The Seer's handmaiden was Jeanette Voiré, grandmother of Theresa Djirrin."

Ryan, who had only been half-listening, perked up. "Excuse me. Are you saying that the handmaiden in the poem is the mother of Tristan's mother's mother?"

Nathan sorted out the sequence. "Yes, or more simply, his great-grandmother."

Ryan was suddenly on his feet. "Tristan! Come here! Quick!"

Ryan's demand was so urgent, Tristan nearly knocked several people over trying to get to the table. "What is it?"

Ryan fumbled around Tristan's neck, groping for the leather cord. "Look, Dad!"

From the leather cord hung the ceramic dove. Gamaliel walked around the table and carefully cut the cord from Tristan's neck, handing the dove to Nathan. Tristan stood upright, rubbing his neck, and gave Ryan a reproachful look. Ryan shrugged and mouthed *Sorry* before turning to watch his father.

Nathan examined the dove from all sides. "It's big enough to hide a key. I suppose there's only one way to find out. Anyone have a hammer?"

One of the men near the table produced a small, metal hammer from the folds of his robe, and Nathan wondered briefly how many of these men were walking tool chests. He set the dove on the table and poised the hammer over it. "Tristan, I want to apologize in advance, in case there's nothing inside."

Tristan nodded. "We must take the chance."

Nathan brought the hammer down, and the dove fractured into hundreds of tiny shards. In the midst of the ceramic debris was a key. The men around the table let out a yell and pounded each other on the back. Nathan handed the key to Klaus. "I believe this honor belongs to you."

Klaus stepped forward almost reverently, taking up the precious box that had for so long been a mystery. Gently he slid the key into the lock. One half turn to the right produced a click, and with a slight pressure, the lid came open. Once again the room was filled with cheers.

Klaus reached inside and pulled out two books and a tattered piece of paper. Nathan leaned in closer so that he could see better.

"The larger book is a hymnal."

"What is a hymnal used for?" Klaus asked.

Millie had never met anyone who didn't know what a hymnal

was. "Some churches use them during worship. It's a book of songs."

Klaus picked up the hymnal and handed it to Gamaliel. Nathan picked up the smaller book and opened it.

"This one is a diary. If, as I suspect, this is Catherine Josiah's, you may find some of the missing pieces to your story."

"What is the piece of paper?" Millie asked softly.

"It's a map," Nathan said slowly, "only there are no names and Scripture verses are the only clues."

Millie looked at Klaus. "Do you know where it leads?"

Klaus nodded. "To the Seer's Treasure. Legend tells of a treasure hidden somewhere underground. Nobody knows what it is, only that Catherine Josiah felt it was important enough to hide it very carefully. We have to assume that she drew the map."

Nathan pulled out a small magnifying glass and examined the map. "Some of these junctions look pretty specific. Have you tried to find the treasure?"

"There are hundreds of miles of tunnels down here. Many attempts have been made. Catherine left some clues in the notebook that is now guarded by Gamaliel. Many have tried to make some sense of them, but until this moment, we did not have the map."

Nathan studied the map again, and his family gathered around to have a look. "Catherine obviously wanted to be sure that whoever found her treasure knew God's Word. Look at the first clue: 'The LORD went before them by day in a pillar of cloud to lead the way. . . .'"

Klaus responded to the question on Nathan's face. "There are hundreds of vents and fumaroles both above and below the ground which might qualify as a pillar of cloud."

Amie was thinking out loud, reading ahead. "Maybe this isn't the clue at all. For each of the Scriptures we're only given the first part. Maybe the second part is meant to be the clue."

Nathan looked at the map again. "The LORD went before them by day in a pillar of cloud to lead the way . . . and a pillar of fire by night,'" he finished. "Mean anything to anybody?"

Klaus looked intently at Gamaliel. "A pillar of fire! The Devil's Spout?"

"It must be!"

A buzz of excitement electrified the room. Klaus finally explained.

"Deep in the mines there is a vertical shaft dug long ago by some poor fools without geotechnical maps. They were hoping to find precious metals to sell behind the company's back, but they hit a reservoir of methane gas instead. Something ignited the gas, the men were incinerated, and the flames rushed into the passage above. Fail-safe charges detonated at the mouth of the passage, sealing it off and it has remained so to this day."

Chris spoke up. "Fail-safe charges don't usually create an airtight seal. What prevents the gas from leaking into the other tunnels?"

"The company sealed the passage off from the main tunnel, but something inside the passage ignites the gas every fifteen minutes or so. Oxygen must be getting in from somewhere. Fortunately, the gas burns before it has a chance to explode. The phenomenon was documented by the engineers who sealed the passage. They called it the Devil's Spout."

Nathan was looking at the map again. "Are there tunnels leading off the shaft?"

"That area was mined pretty heavily, so there's a good chance there are."

"Yes! I see it now. With all respect, Miss Josiah was no draftsman, but these markings before the first clue do look like a vertical shaft. But look here—halfway down there's a passage."

The room was silent for a moment, as everyone was almost afraid to believe they were finally on the path that would lead to the Seer's Treasure.

Klaus looked at Gamaliel. "Assemble a team. You'll need oxygen masks and heat suits."

Nathan interrupted. "Wait a minute, Klaus. If this is as important as you say it is, you should lead the expedition. There may be decisions to be made that only you can make."

Klaus was amused. "I see. And who do you recommend I bring along?"

"Me and my family."

"Your family?"

"Chris is schooled in engineering, among other things, and we are all students of the Bible. All the clues are Scriptures. You might be glad they came along before we're done."

Klaus frowned. "I don't like having children along. It's too dangerous."

"If it's too dangerous for them, it's too dangerous for us," Nathan countered.

Amie cut in. "Besides, if you leave us behind and don't make it, no offense, but I don't really want to spend the rest of my life here."

Klaus laughed out loud, and some of the other men joined him. "Very well. Come along, then."

The group split up and began collecting the equipment and provisions they would need for their expedition. Because of the flurry of activity that followed, and all the haste and excitement involved in the preparations, the Grahams forgot to pray.

The hag lay in her underground chamber on a bed of fetid rags. The shedding of innocent blood always made her giddy, and she had spent the last hour leaping and whirling around the room in devilish glee.

Looking very much like a corpse herself, Saphirra Kraal twitched as she slept, tormented as she always was by hazy images of the past, present, and future. She had paid the Enemy for the power she possessed with her eyes, but such a bargain always comes with a curse.

Her curse was the inability to turn her power off. Even as she slept, jumbled thoughts and pictures tumbled one after the other in an endless stream of information. Only intermittently, when she was wide awake, could she focus enough to glean some hard truth from the morass of chaos in her mind. But there were rare occasions when a thought of intense clarity arrived unbidden, and the clarity of such thoughts was always painful.

The hag convulsed and sat up, staring blindly into the half-darkness of the chamber.

"They live! It's not possible!"

She stood up and wrapped a shawl encrusted with dirt around her shoulders. Grabbing her walking stick, she made her way to the rear of the chamber, groping her way along the wall. When she came to a certain stone, she pressed hard with her cane and the stone sank into the wall, opening a hidden doorway. She slithered through the doorway, like graveclothes upon a foul wind, and the door closed behind her.

Brice Maddock burst in the front door of the Detention Center, his face contorted with rage. The deputy behind the desk jumped to his feet and took several steps backwards.

"Halloch!" Brice bellowed. "Get in here!"

The security chief, Feth Halloch, whacked his leg on his desk and tripped as he scurried out of his office. He had heard that tone of voice before. It was not unheard of for a disloyal security guard to swing from the Judas tree, although contractually such behavior was frowned upon by both companies.

"They're alive, you . . . you . . . idiot!" Brice sputtered.

The chief was aghast. "I don't believe it."

"You want to tell Saphirra that?"

At the mention of the Seer's name, the chief's face turned white.

"Organize as many search squads as it takes, and don't rest until you've found them!" Brice continued, with thinly veiled menace. "While you're at it, look for Sammy Vile. He's missing."

"Yes, sir."

"And one more thing. Post an official proclamation as follows: The traitors from Earth are still at large. If they are not in custody by noon tomorrow, five people will be chosen at random every hour, and hanged by their necks until they are dead. This will continue until the traitors' bodies are delivered, dead or alive."

Brice stormed out of the waiting area, leaving the chief standing speechless.

CHAPTER 5

Chris didn't know how long they had been walking, but his feet were already sore. The problem was not the backpack or equipment he was carrying, but the shoes they had given him. They provided very little support and didn't fit quite right, but Chris didn't want to insult their host by complaining.

In the end there were seven in all in their party, including Klaus, the Grahams, and a hulking behemoth named Asa, who was Gamaliel's assistant. Asa had been designated the keeper of the map.

Everyone was outfitted with heat suits and oxygen masks, which made them look more like hazardous waste handlers than treasure hunters. There had been a brief but heated argument about bringing weapons.

"We need to be able to defend ourselves!" Klaus had said.

"God will defend us," Nathan replied, trying to stay calm.

Klaus was not convinced. "The Lord helps those who help themselves."

"That is not written in the Bible," Nathan answered gently, amazed that the apocryphal platitude had reached even this faraway planet. "Jesus did say, 'He who lives by the sword, will die by the sword'—or words to that effect."

The treasure hunt proceeded without weapons.

Even without swords or guns, the packs and equipment were heavy on their backs, as they trudged through the dark passages.

They were carrying enough food for a week, ropes, explosives, and stonecutting tools, on the chance that the passages had changed since Catherine Josiah wrote the map.

Just when Chris thought his feet might not survive the ordeal, the expedition came to a halt. The passage they were in had run into a dead end. Chris sat down and took his shoes off. Klaus looked back from the front of the group.

"Where's Chris? Oh, there you are. Shoe trouble?"

Chris nodded woefully. "These are killing me."

"Let me have a look."

Klaus walked over and picked up Chris's shoes. Reaching inside, he pulled a liner out of each and reinserted them facing the opposite direction. Chris put them back on and stood up.

"Better?" Klaus asked.

A look of relief passed over Chris's face. "Much! Thank you!"

Klaus returned to the front of the group and pulled a hidden lever. The wall of the dead end slid up into the ceiling, revealing a passage beyond. The group moved forward into the passage and Klaus pulled the slab down behind them until it latched in place. Then he took off his backpack and opened the flap.

"The main tunnel leading to the Devil's Spout is rarely used, so we may not run into anybody. But just in case we better put on our masks. It wouldn't do for the ladies to be noticed."

With oxygen masks in place, the group set off again. A half-hour walk brought them to a tunnel with lights, so they switched off their electric torches. A few minutes later, two miners came down the passage toward the group. Even though their faces were hidden behind masks, the Grahams held their breath as they kept moving.

Klaus nodded as the two men drew near, and one of them spoke.

"Jolly faigreh, neh?"

"Doh neh quando me," Klaus replied. They passed by without incident.

The tunnel they were in merged shortly with a larger thoroughfare, some fifteen feet high and forty feet wide. Railroad tracks ran down one side. Klaus looked back at the group to indicate via hand gestures that they would only be in the tunnel a short while, but all he received were quizzical looks behind the oxygen masks.

He was about to try again, when they happened upon a group of five miners squatting in a circle, evidently taking a break from their work. For a moment, it looked as if the party was going to pass by unnoticed. Then one of the miners spoke directly to Amie.

"De tengo holfogre?"

Amie ignored the man and kept walking, her heart in her throat.

"De tengo holfogre?" he said again, more insistently.

The group stopped, and Klaus interposed himself between the miner and Amie. He spoke quickly and quietly. The Grahams could barely make out the sounds, but it was obviously a warning. When Klaus finished, Asa raised himself to his full height and growled menacingly. The miner raised his hands, clearly apologetic, and the group moved on.

One of the other miners watched them go with a curious expression on his face, then stood up and walked quickly in the other direction.

Another hundred feet brought them to the end of the lights, and they switched on their electric torches. They went on a quarter mile before Klaus signaled to stop.

Chris tapped Klaus on the shoulder. "What happened back there?"

"The fellow thought Amie looked awfully small. 'You have fair hair' is the direct translation. I told him Amie is a dwarf, and that Asa is a close friend who once tore a person's arms off because of an insult."

Ryan interrupted. "Dad, look!"

Set in the stone to their right was a metal door with no handle. Beside it were etched some familiar markings.

Nathan looked down. It was a carving of a fish, made with two opposing arcs joined at the head, and crossing at the other end to make the tail. "It's an ichthus!"

"What's an ixthoose?" Klaus asked.

"I–C–H–T–H–U–S, from the Greek word for fish. It's an early Christian symbol, used as a means of identification," explained Nathan.

Klaus interrupted. "You mean they would carve this symbol in their arms with a knife?"

Nathan laughed. "No. Upon meeting someone in the street, a Christian could make the first arc in the dirt. If the other person completed the fish by making the second arc, they each knew the other was a believer."

Nathan dusted the markings gently with his fingers and examined them closely. "This was done by hand with a chisel. The stroke is too weak to be a man's. It's a good bet this mark was made by Catherine Josiah."

Chris had lifted up his mask and was examining the edges of the door. "How do we get in?"

Klaus flipped back his mask, took off his backpack, and reached inside. "With a drill."

"A drill? It will take forever to get through."

Klaus inserted a long hex-head bit, nearly a foot long and a half-inch thick, into his drill. Moving to the left side of the door, he inserted the bit into a hole in the wall that no one had noticed. As the bit rotated backwards, the door receded into the wall.

Amazed, the Grahams moved into the passage beyond and Klaus repeated the procedure on the other side of the wall, closing the door behind them. The smell of methane was quite strong, and Chris and Klaus both replaced their masks.

Klaus addressed the group. "Everyone stay alert. There's no fast way out."

They moved cautiously along the passage, and a disquieting thought suddenly occurred to Ryan.

"She wouldn't have set traps, would she?"

Klaus stopped to consider the possibility. "It would go against everything I have heard about the Seer Josiah. But let's keep our eyes open."

They walked on further and came to a side passage to the left blocked with rubble. Just inside, another ichthus was carved on the wall. Klaus removed his pack once more and set it down.

"Put on your shoe coverings and check each other to make sure you have no exposed skin. Chris and Asa, as soon as you're ready, please start clearing a crawl space at the top of the rubble. By walking in here, we have brought with us a considerable amount of oxygen. I should warn you: There is some risk of explosion."

Chris finished with his foot coverings and stood up. "You have anything that burns?"

Klaus checked inside his pack. "A plasma welder and a few incendiaries."

"What are the incendiaries for?"

"Manual detonation of explosives and emergency lighting."

"How many do you have?"

"Six. Why?"

"Spread three of them evenly back along this passage and set 'em off. They should burn up the oxygen pretty fast."

"I hate to use them like that."

"It beats getting blown up."

Klaus couldn't argue with that.

Soon the passage was lit brighter than day. The intensity of the light hurt their eyes, but they didn't have to wait long before the flames began to dim and ebb, until the light was a dull red glow.

Chris and Asa set to work on the rubble until they had a crawl space cleared at the top. They climbed back down the rubble and Klaus addressed the group.

"We must wait for the flames, and then move quickly before the cycle repeats itself."

The group split up and waited on either side of the entrance to the side passage. Beyond the pile of rubble, oxygen continued to seep in through cracks and vents in the surrounding rocks, mixing with the methane gas, until the mixture was sufficient to allow combustion. There was a sound like a storm wind outside a window, and flames shot through the crawl space into the passage, licking the far wall. Then they vanished.

Klaus was up the pile of rubble in three bounds and scrambled through the crawl space. Nathan sent Chris next, followed by Amie, Millie, and Ryan. Just before going through himself, Nathan turned to Asa apprehensively, concerned that the giant's massive shoulders might not make it through.

Sure enough, the crawl space was a tight squeeze for Asa, and for a moment he was stuck. Chris stifled a laugh.

"You know, a little axle grease and a pry bar might do the trick."

Asa laughed good naturedly, though it did little to help his situation. Finally with some maneuvering by Klaus, he was able to free his shoulders and he slid on through.

The side passage ended in a mine shaft after about fifty feet. Here and there along the walls appeared to be glowing embers. Chris chipped off a sample with a small pick axe and examined it.

"Looks like lignite. I wish we had a fire hose."

Ryan looked over his shoulder. "Why don't you use some more incendiaries?"

Chris turned to Ryan. "Of course! Little brother, if you weren't wearing a mask, I'd kiss you."

"I'll settle for a handshake," Ryan shot back.

Klaus had already sunk a cleat into the rock and was tying off his rope, when Chris tapped him on the shoulder.

"I need another incendiary."

"What are you talking about? We need to hurry down the rope before the gas ignites again."

"The oxygen flows in from above, right? If we light an incendiary here, it should consume the oxygen before it mixes with the gas. The embers will die out and the flames will be gone for good."

Klaus pulled out an incendiary and handed it to Chris. "I hope you're right about this."

Chris set the device near the edge of the shaft and set the timer for five seconds. Everyone stood back and covered their eyes, as once again, blinding white light filled the surroundings. This time the incendiary dimmed more slowly, and the dimming stopped while there was still a small flame visible. The glowing embers along the wall slowly faded to black. Klaus pulled an oddly shaped cup out of his pack and snuffed the incendiary.

Nathan patted Chris on the back. "Good thinking, son."

Klaus kicked the dead incendiary to one side and nudged the free end of the rope over the edge and down the shaft.

"Now, everyone—down we go. Quick, quick, quick. Asa, I think it best if you go first."

Asa walked over, fitted the rope through two clips on his belt, and spoke for the first time in the Grahams's presence. His voice was rich and well modulated. In another world, he might have been a singer.

"Beauty before age, hmm?"

Klaus didn't miss a beat. "I thought your weight would be a good test for the rope."

"You'd better be smiling under that mask," Asa growled.

Klaus laughed and patted his friend on the shoulder. Asa clipped an electric torch to his belt and slipped over the edge. Nathan stood next to Klaus, and they watched him descend until the light was not much more than a pinpoint. Then his downward motion stopped, and his torch described some complex motions in the dark. Klaus interpreted as he watched.

"He's found the passage . . . all clear . . . the rope is fine." Klaus laughed as he caught the meaning of the last part of the message.

The next person in line happened to be Ryan, and Klaus held out his hand. "You're next."

Ryan clipped himself to the rope, as he had seen Asa do. He squatted to slip over the edge, when a shout came from behind the group.

"You there! What are you doing?"

Klaus moved away from the shaft for a better look. Security guards!

"All of you—*hurry!* I'll handle this," he commanded in a hushed whisper.

He grabbed his backpack, spread his arms out in a welcoming manner, and walked back toward the crawl space.

"Special detachment for Brice Maddock," Klaus said calmly.
"We've heard of no such orders."

Partially hidden by Klaus's body, Ryan slid down the shaft, followed closely by Chris and Amie.

"Our work here is secret, and I suspect your ignorance is deliberate."

"Stop what you're doing or we'll shoot!"

"Go ahead! Then you can explain to Mr. Maddock why his project was delayed."

There was a murmur of conversation on the far side of the crawl space, as Millie began her descent. A moment later the guard in the lead was peering over the pile of rubble again.

"I'm coming through and you'd better have a good explanation!"

He handed his weapon to the man behind him and started through the crawl space. With his protective armor, the guard was almost as broad-shouldered as Asa and struggled into the opening. Klaus darted up the rubble and jammed his backpack into the crawl space with all his might, closing off the entrance to the passage.

Klaus ran back down the passage as the guard, now wedged in, thrashed wildly and shouted a mixture of threats and expletives. Nathan was already over the edge when Klaus clipped himself to the rope.

He dropped like a stone at first, but used his feet to slow his descent and keep from crashing into Nathan, who was going as fast as he could. He could hear the commotion up above, as the guards wrestled to pull their comrade free and then broke through the crawl space all too quickly. Nathan made it to the lower passage just as the first guard reached the top of the shaft.

"Run for it!" Nathan shouted, and the group fled down the passage.

Nathan started after them as Klaus touched down behind him. Instinctively Klaus took three steps and dived face first with his hands over his head. At the top of the shaft, the guard took aim with his laser rifle and fired.

The gas in the shaft ignited, and there was a deafening roar as the explosion rocketed up the shaft, blasting through the upper passage, the rubble, and the metal door beyond. The ceiling collapsed, bringing down several hundred tons of rock on the hapless guards. In a few seconds, the passage and shaft were filled with rubble, closing the Devil's Spout forever.

In the lower passage, the force of the blast had sent the group sprawling headlong, and they lay now very still, in a tangled mass on the floor.

Millie was the first to regain her senses. Her mask was gone, and the acrid smell from the explosion, coupled with the dust that was still settling, was making it difficult to breathe. Still, she was breathing, which meant there must be oxygen.

She rose to her hands and knees, aching all over and ears ringing, and moved cautiously. She seemed to be in fair condition. Some of the others began to stir, and she crawled gingerly over to the smallest body, which she knew to be Amie. Gently she pulled her daughter's mask off. Amie coughed and opened her eyes.

"M-Mom? What happened?"

"Laser blast, I think," Millie replied, checking her daughter for injuries.

Chris sat up, dazed. His head was throbbing painfully. Nathan helped Ryan to his feet and checked on the rest of the family, as Asa stumbled past them looking for Klaus. Klaus lay crumpled up along one wall. Asa stood nearby, unsure what to do. Nathan moved in and started checking vital signs.

"I think he's dead," Asa said numbly.

Chris placed his hand on his shoulder. "Don't be saying that."

Nathan finished his preliminary check. "He's got a pulse. I think his neck is intact. I'm going to take off his mask."

Carefully he pulled the mask from Klaus's face, and found to his relief that the blood was from a superficial cut on his forehead. After making a quick check for broken bones, Nathan motioned for first aid supplies from Millie, who stood anxiously nearby. Carefully he sat Klaus up against the wall and began to dress his minor wounds. Klaus's eyes fluttered open.

"Are you all right?" Nathan asked, still bandaging his head.

"No," Klaus answered thickly, "but I think I'll live."

Nathan knew that in an explosion, a few feet can make all the difference. "You look better than I expected."

"As soon as I hit bottom, I dived to the floor and covered my head. I think my left hand is broken."

Nathan looked down and gently examined Klaus's left arm and hand. There were several bones in the hand broken and Nathan wrapped it as best he knew how. They would have to be set—later. "You've got good instincts," he commented as he worked. "If you'd tried to run, you'd be a dead man."

"Why are we able to breathe?"

"The shaft collapsed. There must be a vent down here somewhere."

Dazed and battered, the members of the group slowly pulled themselves together. Klaus needed Asa's help to walk, and with permission, Nathan took command of the expedition. Asa was not eager to surrender the map, but after some quiet encouragement from his injured friend, he handed it to Nathan.

Surveying the rubble where the entrance to the shaft used to be, Nathan shook his head. "Well, there's no going back. I hope there's another way out."

Another way out. All of a sudden, the realization came to Nathan that they had never prayed for this expedition—not once. It was time to get back on track.

"We need to ask for God's help."

The group slowly huddled together in the cramped passage and joined hands. Chris placed his hand protectively on Klaus's shoulder instead. They prayed in earnest, thanking God for their lives, for His protection and care, and asking Him for His wisdom in completing their quest. Listening to Klaus and Asa pray, Nathan knew without a doubt for the first time that they really served the same Lord.

When they finished, everyone—even Klaus—felt revived. Nathan examined the map by torchlight, verified that everyone was ready, and gave the order to move out. The group fell in behind him single file, trudging along like faithful, wounded soldiers.

* * *

"Explosion off shaft number four, sir!"

Brice was not pleased. "Thank you, that will be all."

"But what are your orders?" the messenger asked, bewildered.

"Execute standard emergency procedures! Now get out!"

Brice hurtled his computer keyboard at the messenger, who left in a hurry. In a high-backed chair, facing Brice's desk, Saphirra Kraal sat brooding.

"I told you."

"You didn't say anything about sabotage!" Brice seethed.

"No. Not sabotage. Something else. Looking for something."

"Give me specifics! I need specifics!"

The Seer's brow furrowed as she tried to concentrate. "They've been hurt . . . some of your men are dead. Standing in a circle . . . ahhhggh!" She grabbed her head and bent double with pain.

"What happened?"

"I lost it."

"Well, get it back!"

"Fool! Not when it goes like that."

Brice slammed his fist down in frustration. "Then get out! You're of no use to me."

Saphirra stood slowly and fixed him with a hideous stare. "Don't order me around, you pasty-faced, crawling little worm."

Brice walked around the desk and placed both hands on her throat. "Let's not forget who's in charge around here, or you might suffer your mother's fate."

Saphirra was unmoved. "And as I'm dragged to the tree, what tales I could tell! Such tales could hang a man."

Brice loosened his grip on the leathery neck and returned to his chair, putting on his silkiest negotiator's voice. "Please inform me if you have any more insights."

He began shuffling the papers officiously on his desk, and when he looked up again, the hag was gone.

The passage that led away from the disaster that used to be the Devil's Spout, gradually broadened until the group was able

89

to walk four abreast. They had just begun to relax in the expanded space, when the passage came to an end. The wall ahead looked like petrified Swiss cheese, with passages large enough to crawl through bored into the rock.

"There must be a dozen passages," Chris observed.

The tunnels seemed to head off in all directions, some beginning as high as six feet off the floor. Nathan pulled out the map.

"The second clue says, 'Therefore God also has highly exalted Him and given Him the name which is above every name. . . .' Any ideas?"

"It says, 'above every name.' Maybe one of the higher passages?" Ryan offered.

Millie shook her head. "No, the first clue was in the form of an antecedent and a consequent."

"A what and a what?" Ryan asked.

"Like a question and answer. The verse is in two parts: the first written, the second not. The second part should be the clue."

Chris frowned. "How does the rest of it go?"

They racked their brains for several long minutes but came up empty. Nathan put a hand to his head.

"What I wouldn't give for a concordance. I guess we'll have to check all the passages and take the best one."

Ryan shone his electric torch down one of the passages. "This one ends after about twenty feet."

Chris checked another. "This one looks passable."

"This one, too," Nathan replied, looking down another.

Millie stood by, trying to complete the Scripture and feeling increasingly helpless. "How can we choose? If we guess wrong, we could be down here a long time."

Asa lifted Ryan so he could get a good look down one of the higher passages, while Amie crouched down and peered into a tunnel at ground level. "I think we could get through this one, but we'd have to crawl on our hands and knees."

Millie's eyes lit up. "*Knees!* That's the rest of the verse! 'That at the name of Jesus every knee should bow . . . and every tongue should confess that Jesus Christ is Lord.'"

Nathan looked at the ground-level passage. "'Every knee should bow.' Looks like we'll have to go on our hands and knees."

"Well, what are we waiting for?" Ryan said.

Nathan walked over to Klaus, who was resting against the wall. "Can you crawl?"

Klaus winced at the thought. "I'm not looking forward to it, but I think I can manage."

One by one the members of the group crawled into the passage, disappearing into the darkness. They went on for what seemed like miles, but in reality was only two hundred feet or so. The going was slow and difficult for Klaus, since he could only use one hand. About a quarter of the way through, Chris maneuvered alongside Klaus to try to provide support, but in the close quarters there wasn't much he could do.

As they continued along, a gentle breeze wafted down the tunnel, which soon became a refreshing wind. They emerged from the passageway into a new chamber, and found their feet sinking into sand as they climbed out. By the light of their torches, they could see this subterranean room was surrounded with tunnels bored into the rock.

"Look at all the holes," Amie said, awestruck. Dozens of passages led off in almost every direction.

"My feet are wet!" cried Millie.

The short, sandy beach they were standing on had disappeared beneath the tide flow of a pool that covered the length and breadth of the room. Wind swirled around the room, creating tiny ripples on the surface of the water. Nathan pulled out the map again and read aloud.

"'Then Moses stretched out his hand over the sea. . . .'"

"That's easy. The parting of the Red Sea," Chris said.

Ryan nodded. He waded boldly into the water, discovering it to be only two feet deep. "What kind of a clue is that? We could walk across without any trouble."

"Yes, but in which direction?" Klaus asked, leaning on Asa.

Millie took the map from Nathan and scrutinized it closely. "I think there's another clue with this one. 'Now on the first day of the week, very early in the morning, they . . . came to the tomb bringing the spices which they had prepared. . . .'"

Amie put her hands on her hips. "Oh, that was a big help."

"Hold it. I think we're getting ahead of ourselves," Nathan countered. "What did they find when they came with the spices?"

Ryan was standing back on shore in a puddle of water. "The tomb was empty."

"The angels said Jesus was alive," Amie added.

Chris looked around the room again. "The stone was rolled away."

"Yes," Nathan said, following his son's gaze, "the stone was rolled away."

Chris waded out into the water, with Nathan close behind. Together they began to examine the wall of the chamber closely. Millie looked at Amie and shrugged. Chris bent down and scraped at the wall with his fingernail.

"Some of the smaller holes are blocked with urethane concrete."

"Why fill only some of the holes?" Nathan mused.

"Beats me. Maybe she was hiding something. Maybe we're supposed to open them all."

"Maybe. Let's keep looking."

They worked their way along the wall until Chris was knocked back by a stream of air coming from one of the smaller holes. Nathan helped to steady him.

Chris smiled sheepishly. "Thanks. I guess that explains the wind."

They continued to the far side of the room, then stopped. Nathan turned back to the group on the beach. "Come here. I want to see if you can make anything out of this."

The group waded across the pool to Nathan and Chris and peered over their shoulders. Set into a hole in the wall about ten inches across was a round stone. The stone was wedged tightly, but tiny jets of air were escaping from around the edges.

"Is this the only stone you've encountered?" Millie asked.

"Yes," Nathan replied. "Several of the other holes were blocked with urethane concrete. This is the only one blocked by a stone."

"It's wedged in there pretty good," Chris observed. "A few good shots with a hammer ought to do the trick."

"Wait a minute. Before we do anything that can't be undone, we should look at the clues again," Nathan cautioned. He closed his eyes, trying to think. "How did the parting of the Red Sea happen?"

Ryan jumped right in. "You saw the video. He raised up his staff and *whoosh!*"

"That's not how it happened in the Bible," Amie replied, frowning. "In Sunday school, the teacher said the video was wrong. Moses only prayed, and God sent a strong wind all night to blow the sea back. The *whoosh* part was only *cinematic affectation.*"

Nathan, who had been momentarily lost in thought, snapped back to the conversation. "Did you say a strong wind?"

Amie nodded, and Chris felt around the edges of the stone. "There's a lot of pressure back there. Like I said, one good shot with a hammer. . . ."

Nathan turned to Klaus. "May I borrow your drill?"

"I'm afraid my drill is currently buried under several hundred tons of rock."

"Oh. Right. Stand back, everyone. I'm going to have to do this the old-fashioned way."

Nathan pulled a pick axe from his pack, and everyone moved off to the side. He swung hard, chipping off some slivers of stone. A second effort produced the same result. His fifth attempt shattered the stone, but a violent stream of air blew the fragments back in his face, tearing his pick axe out of his hand and spinning him backwards into the water.

Chris and Ryan helped their father up and examined him anxiously. Miraculously, he had not been injured by the debris.

"Look!" Millie said, pointing toward the center of the room.

The air jet from the open hole was cutting a swath through the water, almost down to the sediment. The trough made by the piling up of the waters pointed straight to a large hole part way up the opposite wall. After retrieving his pick axe, Nathan led the group across the pond to the hole. The opening was two feet above water level and tall enough to stand in. Ryan climbed up to make sure this was indeed a tunnel, then Asa and Chris helped everyone up.

They made their way quickly along this passage, relieved to be out of the water and the wind. Moments later they found themselves on a wide ledge before a chasm. The walls and floor here were limestone, and the chasm was actually a hole eroded through the floor by water from above.

The shape of the hole created a ledge to the left and one to the right, the one on the left considerably wider. Seventy feet down, clusters of limestone spikes—stalagmites—formed a beautiful, deadly plain for anyone unfortunate enough to lose his or her footing. Nathan read aloud from the map once more.

"'For wide is the gate and broad is the way. . . .'"

Asa, who was weary from carrying his friend, started to the left side. Nathan grabbed his arm and stopped him.

"'. . . that leads to destruction.'"

Asa nodded wearily, as if to convey *I–understand–and–thank–you–but–I'm–too–tired–to–speak*. The group started along the narrow path on the right. The path was so narrow, they had to carry their packs in their hands and edge along single file with their backs against the wall. They were nearly across when Nathan looked to the far side of the chasm and saw that the limestone under the broad path had been washed away. Anyone larger than a small child would have broken through. He thanked the Lord once more for His protection and pressed on.

On the far side of the chasm, the broad limestone passage merged with their path, and Nathan decided this might be a good place to spend the night. Exhausted, the others agreed, so they made camp and prepared a hearty meal. They ate in silence, then stripped off their heat suits and pulled a single lightweight blanket from their packs, Chris and Ryan doubling up to share with Klaus. The torches were turned off, and the group was soon fast asleep.

Nathan awoke in utter darkness some time later, to the sound of an electronic chime. His chronometer had been set as usual for 6:30 A.M., and he had forgotten to turn it off. They had been asleep for almost ten hours. He switched on his torch. Ryan rolled over to shield his eyes, while Amie mumbled something unintelligible. Nathan counted bodies and came up one short. Chris was missing.

He sat up straight and looked hard in both directions. Further on down the passage, he was just able to make out the light from an electric torch. Nathan breathed a sigh of relief, roused the others, and began making breakfast. By the time Chris got back, everyone was up and feeling well fed, well rested, and very sore.

He sat down next to his dad. "We may have trouble up ahead."

"What kind of trouble?"

"A pool of boiling water. I can't find any way across."

Chris ate quickly, while the group put back on their heat suits and finished packing up. Then they moved down the passage. There indeed stood an enormous pool blocking their way. The water was milky gray and boiling, and the limestone seemed to have been eaten away from below by some sort of hot spring. They could just barely see solid ground resume at the far edge of the water.

Nathan shined his light at his feet. "There are numbers carved along the edge."

"I must have missed them," Chris replied.

"Nice detective work, Sherlock," Ryan jibed.

"Go soak your head, runt."

Nathan took out the map. "All right, you two, knock it off. We obviously can't swim for it. Let's see if the map is any help. '. . . Now in the fourth watch of the night Jesus went to them. . . .'"

"Who's *them?*" Ryan asked.

"The disciples, I think," Millie answered.

Chris closed his eyes and put a hand to his forehead. "They weren't separated that often. He always went out to pray early in the morning."

Nathan nodded. "He sent them out ahead of Him to the cities He was going to visit, and after feeding the five thousand, He sent them across the lake."

Chris pointed at his dad. "That's it. He sent them ahead, and then during the fourth watch He came to them walking on the water."

Amie looked at the boiling pool. "It would take a lot of faith to walk across that."

Ryan crouched down to examine the markings. "What do the numbers mean?"

Nathan joined him. "They're obviously a clue of some sort. They seem to be in pairs."

"They could be ranges," Chris added.

Millie picked up the thought. "What was the number in the clue? Four—the fourth watch."

"The fourth watch of the night," Nathan corrected. He stood up so he could see the numbers more clearly. "The second number in each set is three higher than the first: two-dash-five; twelve-dash-three; five-dash-eight; three-dash-six; and nine-dash-twelve. Assuming these are hour designations."

"When was the fourth watch of the night?" Millie asked.

Everyone was silent for a moment, searching their minds for any scraps of information that might help. Then Chris spoke. "When Jesus was crucified, darkness covered the land until about the ninth hour. I remember learning that was three in the afternoon. Count backwards, and their day started at six A.M."

Nathan continued. "If a twelve-hour day ends at six P.M., the first watch of the night would be from six to nine. Let me see: nine to twelve, twelve to three, three to six. The fourth watch would be from three to six."

Chris walked to the right side of the tunnel and stood in front of the spot marked "3–6." He removed a small collapsible shovel from his pack, dropped to one knee, and plunged the end of the shovel into the water. The shovel's downward motion stopped abruptly just below the surface of the water, and there was a resounding clank of metal against stone.

As the others gathered around, he took a step back and began scraping away the limestone where he had been standing. Dark streaks of rock began to appear.

Chris used the shovel to splash some of the hot water from the pool on his miniature excavation, washing away the loose pieces. "A vertical vein of basalt. It must have come up through a crack in the limestone ages ago. When the hot spring washed away the limestone, the basalt was left as a natural bridge. I hope."

"Only we can't see it," Millie observed.

Chris nodded. "It's still going to take faith to get across. Come on."

Using the shovel like a blind man's cane, he took a cautious step out onto the water, gradually putting more weight on his foot until he was standing with both feet submerged a half inch. The illusion that he was standing on the water was uncanny.

"I wish I could get a picture of this," Ryan said.

Nathan smiled a bit. "It would look good on his resume."

Chris took another careful step, and then another, and Ryan followed in his brother's footsteps. Millie went next, then Amie and Nathan. Asa agreed to walk behind Klaus in case he stumbled, but only after assurances from Chris that the basalt would hold his weight.

Klaus and Asa were not halfway across, when Klaus lost his footing. His arms went spread eagle for balance, and Asa reached out to steady his friend. Klaus instinctively turned and grabbed Asa's arm and nearly pulled him into the pool. They clutched each other in an awkward embrace, until Nathan was able to brace Klaus from behind. Klaus let out a *that–was–close* sigh, and followed Nathan the rest of the way across.

With everyone on solid ground again, Nathan surveyed the group. "Everyone okay?"

Everyone responded in the affirmative except Klaus. "I think

I pulled some muscles grappling with that monster back there."

"Kali sabre le viathen vivos salvadas. Ka nugen bretch," Asa said with a touch of sarcasm.

Klaus smiled, and translated. "He says the monster saved my life. The rest I can't repeat as there are children present. Suffice it to say, he thinks me an ungrateful dog of questionable parentage."

They walked on for some time, and the passage narrowed as the limestone slowly gave way to basalt. The ceiling finally became so low that Asa had to walk bent over, and then they came to a fork in the passage. The right passage quickly narrowed to about a foot, while the left broadened and headed upward. Millie had had enough of being underground and hoped secretly they would take the left fork.

Nathan started to the left, but Millie stopped him. "And where do you think you're going?"

"I want to check this out."

"Then kindly leave us the map."

Nathan produced the map and handed it to his wife.

"Mind if I come along?" Chris and Ryan said in unison.

"Not at all."

With torches held out before them like swords, the Graham men hiked up the left passage, which quickly opened out into a vast ocean of darkness. They stopped in their tracks and shined their lights ahead, but there was nothing except an oddly grooved floor, full of pits, that seemed to swallow the light before it could travel very far.

Chris picked up a rock and threw it as hard as he could into the dark, straining forward to hear the impact. The expected sound never came, and somehow the thick silence began to feel suffocating.

"This is not good," Chris said, softly, as if he might disturb some hideous creature inhabiting the darkness.

Nathan picked up a rock and tossed it underhand into one of the nearest pits. The clattering of the rock's descent went on for several seconds, gradually fading to silence. "I hope Catherine Josiah didn't come this way."

"She'd have to be a mountain goat just to make it through the part we can see," Chris replied.

They went back down the passage to the junction, where the rest of the party was waiting. Millie was still studying the map.

"Oh good, you're back. We're having trouble with this clue: 'And the sun became black as sackcloth. . . .'"

Nathan felt his stomach tighten. The dreadful place they had just abandoned was certainly as black as sackcloth.

Chris screwed his eyes shut to think. "It's from Revelation. Judgment Day, the moon turning to blood, all that stuff."

Millie looked at her oldest son patiently. "I don't suppose you remember how it actually goes?"

"'And the sun became black as sackcloth . . . and the moon became like blood. And the stars of heaven fell to the earth,'" Chris finished, not entirely sure he was right.

Nathan felt his stomach tighten some more. It didn't take much imagination to picture those bottomless pits as the final resting place of fallen stars. He turned to his daughter.

"How would you like a little scouting mission?"

Amie's face lit up. "Great!"

"The right passage is pretty narrow. I want you to take off your pack, grab a torch, and tell me what you see."

Amie had her pack off in two seconds, put torch in hand, and headed for the crevice. Turning sideways, she slipped through without problem and disappeared from view. A few moments later, they heard her voice excitedly on the other side.

"Oh, Daddy! It's the stars! The stars that fell from the sky!"

Nathan squeezed through the crevice after his daughter. He saw immediately the reason for Amie's excitement. Scattered across the room in waves of rolling hills were shiny nuggets of metallic rock. Forty feet above, the ceiling twinkled overhead as well.

Chris came up behind his dad. "Wild. Is that galena?"

"It looks like it, but I've never heard of it piling up like this."

Chris instinctively picked up a piece and stuck it in his pocket. He could have it analyzed, assuming they ever got out of here and made it back to Earth. As the other members of the group joined Nathan and Chris, hauling the backpacks, Amie called down from a pile near the center of the room.

"I can't see any other exits from up here!"

Nathan and the others joined Amie atop her heap. "It's probably buried. Everyone spread out and start searching along the edges."

The members of the group moved out to roughly equal distances along the wall and started looking for a possible passage. Chris found a promising indentation, pulled out his shovel, and started digging, but soon discovered that it was only an alcove. Then Amie cried out again.

"Hey everybody, I think I fou—"

As the others watched helplessly, her arms shot upward and she dropped from sight. Scrambling to the spot where she had vanished, they found an opening into a steep diagonal passage nearly filled with the shiny rocks. Chris and Nathan pulled out their shovels and dug like madmen to widen the hole.

"Amie! Are you all right?" Nathan yelled.

Faintly her voice came from below. "I'm okay! But my torch is broken!"

Nathan looked at Chris. "Do you mind?"

Chris's face broke into a grin. "Not at all. Amie! Clear the way, I'm coming down!"

Clutching his shovel determinedly, he took a step forward and dropped down the hole, sliding quickly out of sight around a bend in the passage. Using the tool to maneuver, he plummeted downward on a slide of glittering pebbles. Nathan opened his mouth too late.

"Idiot child. He could have used a rope."

Chris hit the bottom at high speed and skidded across the floor, finally coming to a rest near the center of another chamber. The first thing he noticed was a hazy cloud of steam that filled the top half of the room. Scanning the walls, he discovered several passages leading off in different directions. Amie helped him up.

"That was some ride!" Chris said, still a little dizzy from the experience.

Amie did not share his enthusiasm. "It's scary when you don't know what's coming."

Chris hollered up that he was okay, and Nathan took out his rope. There was no suitable outcropping of rock available to tie it off, so Asa drove a spike into the wall, and Nathan attached his rope to that. The trip down was slippery, but the group was soon assembled in the lower chamber, none the worse for the descent.

Millie gave Amie a reassuring hug and read again from the map. " 'We who are alive and remain. . . .' "

She looked around the group for help but received only blank stares. "Oh, come on. Somebody must know the rest of it." No response. "All right. We'll do it the hard way." She looked at Chris. "Probable context?"

"Doesn't sound like anything in the Old Testament," Chris offered.

Ryan spoke next. "Sounds more like the end times."

"There's that prophetic stuff in Daniel," Amie added.

Nathan split the verse up in his mind. "Assuming it is the end times, what happens to those of us who are 'alive and remain'?"

"We'll be caught up to meet the Lord in the air!" Amie said, excitedly.

"There are passages along the wall," Chris said, thinking aloud. "Any one of them might take us upwards."

Nathan looked around. "All I see is steam. Chris and Ryan, go and see if you can find the source of the steam. The rest of you split up and see which of the passages goes up."

Chris and Ryan ducked down so they could see where they were going and moved toward the far side of the room. The rest of the group fanned out and began exploring passages. The source of the steam proved to be very strange indeed. Someone had deliberately cut a hole into the side of a vent which ran vertically and parallel to the chamber they were standing in.

"Dad! Come over here!" called Chris.

Nathan appeared out of the steam, followed by the others. "What have you got?"

Chris ran his fingers over the markings surrounding the crude hole. "Someone cut a hole into this vent with a pick axe."

"Why cut into a vent?"

"Either to let the steam out . . ."

". . . or let someone in."

Klaus stepped forward. "The tunnel we checked was a dead end. Maybe there was no other way out, and she had to open the vent with her pick axe."

Nathan looked at the billowing clouds roiling upwards. "We'll have to repair the heat suits."

It was true. Everyone in the group had rips and tears in their suits from the explosion and their travel along the way, any of which might allow the scalding steam to penetrate to their skin. Klaus took two rolls of heat-resistant tape from Nathan's pack. He and Asa went from person to person, patching holes until they couldn't find any more, then they did the same for each other.

Nathan stepped through the hole and started to climb, but the steam was buffeting his body so hard, he couldn't hold onto the rocks. He clawed his way back out into the chamber, panting.

"Can't . . . hang on. . . . The turbulence. . . ."

Asa stepped forward. "I will block the steam." He put his arms over his head and leaned forward as far as he could across the hole. The upper torso of his suit took a terrible beating, but he stood firm and much of the force of the steam was deflected.

Nathan put his hand on Chris's arm. "Look after your sister. Millie, keep right behind me."

Chris nodded, and Nathan crawled over Asa and started his ascent. Millie stepped out, following Nathan carefully. The rocks were slippery, but the craggy walls of the vent were replete with good hand holds, and Nathan was able to move upward with some confidence.

Nathan guessed they had climbed some fifty feet when they came to a ledge that had been hewn out of the wall by hand.

Apparently, Catherine Josiah had needed a place to rest, and had made one for herself. Everyone in the group was thankful for the wide ledge, as the climb was becoming difficult. Asa had started upward, and clouds of steam were blowing full force up the vent again.

Breathing deeply, Ryan took a good look at his surroundings and noticed, through the thick clouds of steam, that the wall behind the ledge was split horizontally by a fissure about twelve feet wide and eighteen inches high. Nathan took the map back from Millie and shouted over the roar of the steam.

"The map ends here, but there are three more clues. The first one says, 'It is easier for a camel to go through the eye of a needle. . . .'"

Millie knew this one immediately. "'. . . than for a rich man to enter the kingdom of God.' But what does it mean?"

Nathan leaned over and looked into the fissure. "I think it means we're going through here on our bellies. And we have to leave our packs behind."

Chris shined his light inside. The new passage stretched back quite a way. "We need those packs."

"There is another problem," Klaus interrupted. "Asa will not go that way. He was nearly crushed a few years back when a tunnel collapsed. It took the rescuers fourteen hours to dig him out. A tight space like this will paralyze his mind with fear. If he freezes up in there, I don't think we could pull him out."

Asa sat silently, but it was evident his mind was made up. Chris spoke first. "Then you'll have to keep climbing. There's a good chance the vent is open at the top."

"If not, we'll have to come back later and dig you out," Nathan said soberly.

"You can't just leave him here!" Amie protested.

"He'll be all right, *Liebchen*," Nathan replied. "Besides, Asa, you may be out before we are!"

The travelers discarded their packs and arranged them on the ledge, in case they were needed later. Then the Grahams and Klaus laid hands on Asa, praying for his safety. Once Klaus had hugged his friend and said good-bye, he and the Grahams wedged their bodies into the fissure, scooting along a few inches at a time, until they all had disappeared from view. Asa watched them go and shuddered, then turned and continued his climb up the vent.

CHAPTER 6

Above ground it was midmorning, although the drab, ubiquitous lighting inside the dome gave no indication of a new day. Inside Brice Maddock's office, Halton Maddock was trying to avoid a shouting match with his son.

"I just want to know why security is on full alert, that's all," Halton said with exaggerated calm.

"I told you, the Grahams escaped from the Detention Center and some of the bargaining units are using it as an excuse to challenge our authority."

"Can't we meet with them?"

"They're too emotional right now. Things should quiet down in a few days. Until then, the full alert is necessary. Now, if we can change the subject, I need your help with something."

"What is it?"

"Our last shipment was several hundred tons short. The customer is pretty irate. I told him you would call."

"It's always something. What happened?" Halton asked, shaking his head.

"We traced it to an error on one of the manifests."

As he had a thousand times before, Halton capitulated to circumstance without questioning his son's story. "I'll handle it."

Without another word, he turned and walked out. Brice smiled imperceptibly. The shortage on the last shipment was merely another in a long string of carefully orchestrated crises designed and implemented by Brice to, as he put it, "keep the old man busy."

Brice picked up his communicator and called Halloch, the security chief. "Round up five people for the Judas tree."

"But who do you want?"

"It doesn't matter, so long as it's not anyone the townspeople already want dead. We need a suitable example. Be sure to include some women and children."

There was a long pause on the other end, before the security chief responded, and he made no effort to keep the revulsion out of his voice. "Yes, sir."

Brice terminated the connection, and sat back in his chair to consider the unfolding of his plans over the next twenty-four hours. Everything seemed to be going perfectly, but he needed assurance. He stood up, walked over to his door, and locked it. Returning to his desk, he reached under the front edge and pressed a secret button. A hidden panel slid open in the wall behind him, revealing a stairway. He stepped through and pressed another button on the wall, closing the door behind him.

Nathan's arms and legs were screaming with fatigue. He kept moving, partly because something inside told him time was running out and partly because he didn't like tight spaces much more than Asa. Klaus was keeping up, despite his wounded hand, and Chris and Ryan were faring pretty well. Millie and Amie had decided to throw appearance to the wind and crawl flat on their stomachs, and seemed to be having the easiest time of all.

Carrying the torches by hand had proven impossible, and the skewed lighting produced by clipping them on their belts was confusing. So they crawled on in darkness. Chris was wondering how long they would have to go on, when he caught a glimpse of light up ahead.

"Is that daylight?"

Nathan, who had turned his face to one side to give his neck a rest, looked forward. Not more than fifty feet ahead, the fissure came to an end, and he could see—he was almost afraid to hope—daylight.

"I sure hope so."

The group pressed on with renewed vigor, and soon emerged in a round room some fifteen feet high, with a spongy carpet of dark, green moss. The ceiling overhead had a long crack, through which daylight was streaming, and they could see trees beyond. The walls were made of brick, and there was a mound about six feet high on the far side of the room.

Klaus suddenly recognized where he was. "This must be one of the old cisterns on Beggars' Hill."

"That would explain the bricks and the moss," Chris agreed.

Amie was curious. "The moss?"

Millie put a hand on her daughter's shoulder. "Moss grows best where it's damp. If there was any moisture in the air, it would collect down here."

"What does the next clue say?" Chris asked.

Nathan looked at the well-worn map once again. "'And there were shepherds abiding in their fields . . .'"

Millie snapped her fingers. "It's the recitative from Handel's *Messiah*. Forgive me, but I can't remember the words unless I sing it."

Klaus looked on with bemused awe, as the lovely sound of Millie's voice filled the cistern.

"'And there were shepherds abiding in their fields, keeping watch over their flocks by night.'"

As the last note echoed away, no one wanted to speak and break the spell. At last, Nathan spoke almost in a whisper.

"That was beautiful, but what does it mean?"

Amie looked down. "Well, the moss does look kind of like a field."

"But I don't see any sheep," Nathan replied.

Chris looked around the group. "Sure you do. What are we, if not sheep?"

"And where would you stand to watch over us?" Ryan asked.

In unison every head turned to look at the mound. Chris walked soundlessly across the moss covered floor and ascended the small hill. From the top, he could jump and touch the ceiling, but that wasn't necessary. There was a ladder set into the wall, and a hatch overhead.

Chris dropped to his knees and began to examine the moss at the top of the mound for anything unusual. Ryan began to check the bricks behind his brother. The others searched the base of the mound for any clue how they might proceed.

Ryan found his attention drawn to one brick in particular. "Chris, does this look like mortar to you?"

Chris ran his fingers around the brick in question. "That's dirt." He took out his pocket knife and began chipping away. The dirt proved to be only two inches deep and the brick came loose easily. Chris stopped and turned to Ryan.

"Here, little brother. You found it, you take it out."

Ryan thought this a marvelous idea. He pulled the brick out of the wall and held it up. In the top of the brick was etched an ichthus. He handed the brick to his brother, reached inside the hole in the wall, and withdrew a worn piece of paper.

"'Where your treasure is . . . ,'" he read.

Several members of the family had heard this repeatedly as a sermon topic, and so all spoke up at once. "'. . . there your heart will be also.'"

Their triumphant smiles gradually faded, as they realized they had no idea what the clue referred to. For lack of a better suggestion, Nathan suggested everyone spread out and look for something with a heart on it.

While everyone else combed the floor and walls for some sign of a heart, Ryan sat down on the mound with the brick. Tracing the carved fish emblem with his finger, he watched his family and Klaus search the cistern.

He found his mind wandering, and he said a prayer for Asa and thought about fish. Then he returned his attention to the brick and began trying to remember "heart" references from the Bible. *Love the Lord with all your heart . . . God hardened Pharaoh's heart . . . trust in the Lord with all your heart . . . Jesus died of a broken heart on the cross. The cross. . . . The* light from the crack in the ceiling was shining down on the floor, intersecting a ridge made by a tree root in the floor. *A cross.*

Ryan walked over to his father, who was scraping lichen off the wall to look at the bricks.

"Dad, Catherine Josiah was a Christian, right?"

Nathan didn't look up. "Yes."

"You and Mom told me that when you become a Christian, you bring all of your cares, emotions, desires—your heart—and leave it at the foot of the cross, right?"

"That's right. Why do you ask?"

"I found a cross."

Nathan stopped scraping. "Where?"

"Right there." Ryan pointed to the spot where the jagged band of light crossed the ridge. Nathan walked over and stared at the ground. Chris turned from where he was working on his hands and knees. "What's up?"

Nathan motioned him over. "You see the cross where the light intersects that small ridge? Your brother thinks that may be the marker we're looking for."

"Hmm. I don't see how it relates to the clue."

"You know the concept of leaving your heart at the foot of the cross. State it as a proposition: *The cross is where the Christian's heart is.* If it's true that wherever your treasure is, there your heart is, then surely the converse is true."

"Wherever your heart is, there your treasure is?"

Chris knelt and set to work with his digging tool. One by one, the others gathered around.

"Find something?" Millie asked.

Chris kept digging. "Ryan did. I'm just testing his theory."

He only had to dig a few inches before his tool struck something soft. Nathan and Ryan helped clear away the moist dirt and moss, while the others looked on with intense curiosity. Chris pulled something bulky out of the hole.

"It's a sort of backpack," Klaus said, wondering if this drab fabric bag could really be the Seer's Treasure.

"How was she able to get her pack through, when we had to leave ours behind?" Amie asked.

Chris looked down at the bag. "It's a little smaller. I don't know. Maybe she found this place and came back later through the hatch."

"It's very possible she knew about this place long before leaving her pack here. Theresa Djirrin told me Catherine used to play in the tunnels as a child," Klaus explained.

Millie couldn't stand the suspense any longer. "Well, aren't you going to open it?"

Chris unbuckled the straps, threw open the flap, and spread the contents out on the moss. For a moment, Ryan thought they had found someone's old school bag by mistake.

"Books? The Seer's Treasure is books?" he asked in disappointment.

Klaus smiled, never taking his eyes off the items on the moss. "To a people starved for knowledge, these are worth far more than any gold or jewels."

Nathan looked up. "Starved for knowledge? I don't understand."

"It's another part of our history, Nathan—something we don't like to talk about. After Catherine disappeared, the company closed down the schools and confiscated all the books. The people revolted at first, but a few public executions quickly broke down their resistance. Anyone found teaching their children, or anyone else for that matter, was set to hard labor deep in the mines."

Nathan shook his head in disgust. "It's a page right out of Earth's history. Tyrants withholding education as a way to control the people."

"It has worked very well with us. We are a broken people, with precious little to look forward to except a life of hardship and the mines. We are ignorant and know it, which makes us very suspicious of what outsiders might do to us. What little knowledge we have is passed down orally within the Brotherhood."

"But you seem pretty knowledgeable to me," said Chris.

"About equipment and explosives, yes, but you may have noticed how little I had to offer to your discussions on this expedition."

"You speak English very well, and I know it isn't your native tongue," Millie said encouragingly.

"English is the language of the enemy, the language of the company. They teach it while you learn a skill for the mines. My native tongue is a chaotic mixture of eleven different languages. When you work side by side with someone who speaks another language, day after day, year after year, you begin to learn some of his words. They become part of your language and are passed on to your children. Pretty soon, you have four or five different words for *shovel* and you use them interchangeably."

The light was beginning to dawn for Nathan. "I think I get it. We once hosted a German exchange student and a Spanish student, and they both spoke three languages. When they couldn't think of a word in one language, they jumped to another. Their conversations were the most jumbled hodge-podge of gibberish I ever heard."

"It is the same for us, only worse."

Chris started going through the books. "*Fundamentals of Math . . . World History . . . Basic Economics . . .* hey, Klaus! Here's a Bible."

Chris handed the Bible to Klaus, who received it with almost childlike wonder. But as he opened the worn cover, his face took on a pained expression. "It's in English."

Nathan spoke gently. "You have to stop thinking of English as the language of your enemy. It was probably Catherine Josiah's native tongue."

Klaus's expression softened. He clutched the Bible to his chest and tears welled up in his eyes. "Thank you."

Under the last book, Chris found a sealed plastic pouch. "Dad, there's something else here."

Nathan opened the pouch and removed the papers inside. He examined the documents for a moment. "*Interstellar Trade Commission,*" he read, and turned to the last page. "Signed by

111

Terrence Maddock." Turning back to the first page, he began scanning the information.

On the third page, he stopped, amazed.

"What is it?" Millie asked.

Nathan handed her the document. "I don't believe it. Read the part circled in red."

Millie cleared her throat. "'In the event of undue hardship, wherein the parties find it necessary to sell their shares back to the company in order to sustain life and limb, the company shall hold such shares in trust, until such time as the parties are able and willing to purchase said shares back from the company. Should the period during which the company is trustee of said shares exceed fifty years, ownership of said shares shall revert to the original owner, his or her descendant or beneficiary.'"

Klaus was confused by the legal jargon. "What does that mean?"

With the same incredulous look on his face, Nathan replied, "It means that you, your Brotherhood, and all the people in town are the rightful owners of the mining operations."

Klaus was speechless. Chris started thinking out loud. "That must be what Catherine was using against Terrence Maddock. When she got wind of the plot against her, she must have hidden the document here, along with the books. But what happened to her?"

Klaus found his voice. "I don't know, but we have to get this back to the Brotherhood right away."

It was a ragged, filthy, exhausted little group that shuffled into the main meeting room of the Brotherhood an hour later. News that the Seer's Treasure had been found spread through the Brotherhood like wildfire, and they were inundated by an enthusiastic crowd of well-wishers who had managed to slip away from their daily routines. When Asa had returned alone, they had expected the worst. It was with great relief that the Brotherhood welcomed back their leader and newest members.

Once the provisions of the Trade Commission document were explained to the Brotherhood, the members were ready to find

112

Halton Maddock and confront him. Gamaliel stood before the gathering and held up a hand until the buzz of excited conversation was quiet.

"We have a more pressing issue to consider. As you know, five innocent people are scheduled to hang today. A short time ago I discovered that Tristan Djirrin and his mother are among them."

"What are they charged with?" Klaus asked, outraged.

"Nothing. There is no charge. Brice Maddock is trying to pressure the people to hand over the family from Earth."

After the success of the rescue, Ryan couldn't believe what he was hearing. "How does he know we're alive?"

"Brice is probably in close contact with Saphirra. She might know," Nathan suggested.

Klaus agreed. "Aye, she might. This changes things, it does."

Nathan addressed Gamaliel. "When are the hangings scheduled?"

"Twelve noon."

"It's almost ten o'clock already! Why didn't you do something?"

Gamaliel stepped back, abashed. "Klaus was gone. Hooded robes have been forbidden. The guards have orders to shoot to kill." The priest looked devastated. "Forgive me, I have no gift for strategy."

Nathan felt like a heel. "I'm sorry. I didn't mean that the way it sounded. But isn't there something we can do?"

Klaus massaged his forehead with his good hand, perplexed. "It sounds like a rescue is out of the question. I don't see any options."

Klaus's use of the word *options* struck a chord deep inside Nathan, and his mind kicked into planning mode, even though he was exhausted. He signaled for Klaus to sit down at the table and then joined him. The room was wall-to-wall people, waiting expectantly.

"There are always options. First, we can do nothing—and five innocent people will die. More than that, Brice will probably make good on his plan to murder his father. With Brice in control, the situation will continue to deteriorate here, and the security force will be free to hunt down the Brotherhood."

"That isn't an option," Klaus said firmly.

Nathan continued. "Or, we can do something. We can try to get the Interstellar Trading Commission document in front of Halton Maddock. We can try to get a message to Earth. And we can try to save those people."

Klaus looked at Nathan as if he were mad, but a smile of hope played at the corners of his mouth. "That doesn't give us much time. What do you suggest?"

"We need a diversion."

"I'm afraid I used most of my explosives during your rescue. I doubt we could get close to the square anyway. The guards are out in force."

"Do you have any general alarm?"

"There's a horn in the square, but the people will already be gathered."

Chris piped up. "Aren't these domes equipped with some kind of warning system, in case the air starts to go bad or the surface of the dome becomes compromised?"

"There's an environmental monitoring station behind the Administration Building. I've seen horns on top, but I don't even know if they work."

"We'll have to take that chance." Nathan turned to the group, knowing it would take every person in the room to accomplish what he had in mind. "I have a plan, but it's going to be all or nothing."

Klaus closed his eyes, trying to ignore the pain in his hand. "Let's hear it."

"All right. Klaus, you take Chris and two of your men—dressed as a work party—up to the environmental monitoring station. If the thing has an alarm, it must have a test mode. Chris, you should be able to set it off manually, if the test mode doesn't work.

"I will take Millie and Amie up to the Administration Building. They don't have pictures of us, so we might not be recognized, and there's a chance we'll be mistaken for employees.

Once inside, Millie and Amie will locate the communications room and send a message to Earth, while I locate Halton Maddock and brief him on the document we uncovered. If he's the man of integrity I think he is, we have a chance. If not, we may be sunk.

"If we're successful, there may be an interim period when the guards don't know who's the boss. We need to do something to even the odds. What will the security guards do when the alarm goes off?"

Klaus shrugged. "They'll be expecting another rescue attempt. Chances are they'll herd the prisoners back into the Detention Center."

"Do you have any dirt-moving equipment?"

"There are a couple of scrappers outside shaft number five."

"What's a scrapper?"

"A hefty machine with treads and a big shovel on the front."

"Sounds like a front-end loader. Is there any way to get them into the square?"

"You can drive them right down Baker's Chute. It runs into an alley that feeds into the square." Klaus looked at one of the men for confirmation, and received a nod. "But the Brotherhood has no one who can operate them."

"Dad?" Ryan volunteered. "One of the guys taught me how to use a front-end loader when I was working construction."

Nathan shook his head. "Thanks, but I'm not sure that's such a good idea."

"The controls can't be that different. They were designed for a human, right?"

"And if you get caught in a fire fight, do you think you can learn the controls under heavy laser fire?"

"If there's a fire fight, I'll be too busy diving for cover to learn anything."

"Good answer." Nathan mulled over the offer for a moment, and then turned to Klaus. "Are you sure you don't have anyone who can drive?"

Asa stepped forward. "I have experience with some heavy equipment. I might be able to learn."

Nathan was ill at ease but saw he had no choice. "Well, okay. Asa, you take Ryan and two of your best men to shaft number five. Take the scrappers down to the square and block the doors to the Detention Center; then get out of there fast. You might not meet any resistance before you reach the square, but at the first sign of trouble, you clear out." He faced Klaus again. "Do we have any weapons or munitions?"

"Three laser rifles, a few incendiaries, and about a pound of explosives."

"We'll give two rifles to Asa's team, one rifle and half the explosives to Klaus, and I'll take the other half. We can split up the incendiaries evenly. We don't want to kill anybody. If we fail, we retreat."

Ryan stepped up to the table. "Dad, with the doors to the Detention Center blocked, what's to stop them from executing the prisoners?"

"It is a risk, but my guess is they'll be too busy trying to get out. More likely, they may decide to keep them as hostages until they know what's going on."

Klaus spoke again. "What if Halton Maddock sides with his son?"

"If we're successful in getting a message to Earth, I don't see how he can."

"Why? Any help from Earth will take at least two weeks to arrive."

"True. But if the Interplanetary Police are on their way, what would you want them to find when they arrive? Piles of dead bodies and a town in flames?"

Klaus nodded. He paused for a moment, obviously deep in thought. Then he stood and looked around the room as he spoke, verifying that he was speaking for all of them. "This may be the only chance we ever get to break free. I pledge to you my life and the lives of the Brotherhood." He bowed his head in simple prayer. "May God have mercy on our souls."

Outside the Detention Center, all was quiet. The townspeople were beginning to gather in somber silence to view the spectacle now only an hour away. Inside, the five doomed prisoners sat quietly in their cell, grimly awaiting the inevitable. Only Tristan and his mother held out any hope of being saved, as they continued to pray for the Lord's deliverance.

Out front in the receiving area, Brice Maddock was pacing back and forth, barking questions at the security chief.

"How can five squads spend three days searching every square inch of this dome and not find any sign of Sammy Vile?"

"He might be underground, but that would take an entire legion six months to find him."

"Why is it you can't seem to do anything I ask? I wanted Nathan Graham dead. You failed at that. I wanted Sammy Vile found, and you failed at that. I'm going to give you another chance. Today, just before the hangings, I'm going to denounce my father to the townspeople. They will probably riot and storm the Administration Building. Let them. When he sees them coming, he will flee to his emergency tube car. When he presses the button, the failsafe on the purge circuits will be disabled, and his car will be blown out of the dome. With my father's untimely demise, I will take over the corporation. The transition will be difficult, and I am going to need your support."

The chief was silent for a moment, his face sour. "The answer is no. So long as your father's in charge, I report to him. You strut around here like you own the place. Well, you don't. I knew you were a vicious brat without a shred of human decency, but I didn't think you'd murder your own father. You disgust me."

Brice's expression never changed as he calmly walked over to the chief's adjutant, drew his pistol out of his holster, aimed it at the chief, and pulled the trigger. The chief collapsed, dead before he hit the floor. Brice walked over to the body and smiled sardonically.

"Revolution sometimes requires difficult choices, my friend."

Brice walked back to the adjutant and handed him his pistol.

"Congratulations on your promotion. I trust I can count on you to carry out my orders."

Eyes riveted on the still form on the floor, the new chief nodded.

"Good. Now, close your mouth and get back to work." Brice headed toward the door, and almost as an afterthought, turned and waved a hand at the body. "And clean that up while you're at it."

The three strike teams had taken twenty minutes to equip themselves, dress in work clothes, and meet back in the main meeting chamber. Chris was busy giving a crash course in the workings of a laser rifle, while Nathan and Klaus discussed final details. After several minutes of serious prayer for the mission, the group moved out into the main passage and prepared to split up.

Nathan addressed the group. "This day is the Lord's. Win or lose, we belong to Him."

There was a murmur of general agreement. Ryan said good-bye to his family, and Asa's group headed down one passage, while Nathan's and Klaus's teams headed down another. Within ten minutes they came to a junction with a side passage and Klaus brought the two groups to a halt.

"Nathan, take your team down here. In a quarter mile, you will come to a ladder. The exit should put you downhill and to the left of the Administration Building."

Nathan nodded and shook Klaus's hand. "Watch yourselves out there."

Chris said good-bye to his folks and Amie. "Keep your head down, squirt."

Amie smiled, and it was clear that in the innocence of youth, she was probably the calmest member of the group. Impulsively, she reached out and hugged him, then turned and rejoined her parents.

Nathan led his wife and daughter down the side passage, and Chris watched them go until they were out of sight. For the first time it occurred to him that he might never see them again—or at least not in this life. He began to get misty-eyed; then he shook himself. He couldn't afford to think like that now. There was too much at stake.

Klaus led Chris and the remaining two men onward for another five minutes until the passage came to an end. The ladder up the right sidewall looked as if it had not been used in a long time. Chris looked to Klaus and remembered Asa's words from deep in the tunnels.

"Age before beauty."

Klaus started up the ladder without missing a beat. "Nay, 'tis wisdom before foolishness."

Chris found it a bit awkward climbing with a laser rifle slung over his shoulder, but he finally hit upon a way of turning his body so that the gun hung free. When they reached the top, Klaus undid the latches and threw open the hatch, with no apparent concern for being seen by anyone on the surface. When Chris climbed out, he saw why.

The exit was in a small clearing surrounded by thick foliage, and the hatch was designed to look like a tree stump. Klaus closed the hatch and looked around to get his bearings. After a moment, he headed quietly off through the dense undergrowth, motioning for the others to follow.

Shortly they were able to see the environmental monitoring station through the trees. The building was nondescript—a shack really—with two large horns on top, surrounded by a concrete wall, and located at the top of a hill adjacent to the dome wall. At the foot of the hill, about thirty feet from the edge of the woods, was a shiny metal shed.

Klaus started out of the woods toward the foot of the hill. In the same moment Chris spotted two guards behind the station wall, taking aim. Chris grabbed Klaus by the collar and jerked him back into the woods, throwing him to the ground. Klaus opened his mouth to protest when the air around them was filled with sizzling bursts of laser fire. The foursome crawled on their hands and knees deeper back into the woods and paused to rest, well out of view of the guards on the hill.

"Who puts guards on an EM station?" Chris asked, exasperated.

Klaus shrugged. "Why not?"

More laser blasts penetrated the woods nearby, and they retreated further into the underbrush.

Chris spoke again, this time in a whisper. "There's no way we're going to make it up that hill alive."

Klaus checked Chris's chronometer.

"We've got five minutes to come up with another plan, or we'll have to try."

The ladder turned out to be right where Klaus promised it would be, and after a short climb, Nathan, Millie, and Amie emerged from the shaft into a large, hollow log. They crawled out of the log and found themselves in some fairly dense woods. Nathan worked his way uphill and to the right as quietly as he could, looking back every few steps to make sure Millie and Amie were keeping up.

Soon the top of the Administration Building was visible through the trees, and they kept moving until they had the front doors in sight. Two guards were standing on either side of the doors. Nathan crouched low and signaled for the others to do the same.

"What do we do now?" Amie whispered.

"Pray that Klaus and Chris set off that alarm."

Asa's team exited the underground into the woods and walked through the trees until they came to a thicket, just below the clearing outside the entrance to mine shaft number five. Asa and Ryan peeked over the berm at the edge of the clearing. The two scrappers sat idle on either side of the mine entrance, and a road exited to the right toward town.

Two guards stood near the entrance, clearly bored and feeling sorry for themselves. The mine watch was at the bottom of the roster, and usually reserved for the losers on the squad. Asa slipped his laser rifle off his shoulder.

"What are you doing?" Ryan whispered.

"I'll push them back into the mine long enough for you to get one of the scrappers going."

"I have a better idea."

Ryan ducked down and grabbed a rock about half the size of a baseball from the berm. Making sure he was out of sight, he drew his arm back and threw the rock high over the clearing into the woods beyond the mine entrance. The rock landed with a leafy clatter, and both guards turned toward the sound.

"What was that?"

"I don't know."

"You'd better go check it out."

"You check it out. I'm staying here."

Ryan let fly with another rock. The guards were becoming increasingly nervous.

"All right, wise guy. You check out that one; I'll check out the first one."

"It's probably just an animal."

"You moron. The only animals around here are people. You wanna get out-flanked?"

The guards disappeared into the woods.

"Give me one of the incendiaries," hissed Ryan.

Asa was mystified, but so far the plan seemed to be working. Ryan ran on tiptoe out into the clearing, set the fuse for thirty seconds, and threw the incendiary as hard as he could exactly between the points where the guards had entered the woods. The device crashed through the canopy of trees a hundred feet away and hit the ground with a thud.

Ryan turned and signaled for Asa to take the scrapper on the left side of the mine entrance, and then ran to the other. Asa passed his rifle to one of his team and the two men jogged across the clearing. The last man, also carrying a rifle, ran to Ryan's side. Ryan climbed up into the cab of the scrapper, told his companion to stand guard behind the cab, and started studying the controls.

Even at that moment he heard the unmistakable hiss of flame from the incendiary as it ignited. The sound was followed immediately by laser fire, then answering fire from the same part of the woods. The firing broke for a moment, and someone shouted.

"Hold your fire, you idiot! It's me!"

Ryan waved his hand at Asa and punched the starter button, and the engine roared to life. Asa did the same, and both scrappers began rumbling toward the road. Ryan was already out of the clearing, with Asa close behind, when guards came bursting out of the woods, guns blazing. One of them pulled a communicator from his belt.

Both gunners on the scrappers opened fire. The guards dived and rolled into the clearing, and the communicator went flying. Asa's gunner fired again, chewing up the dirt in front of the guards. The two crawled frantically toward the mine, desperately seeking cover. Ryan saw them disappear into the entrance and cut his engine.

"Go for the supports!" he yelled, leaning out of the cab.

Both gunners fired, concentrating several long bursts on the main supports of the mine entrance. The ceiling collapsed in a cloud of dirt and rubble, sealing the guards inside the mine.

"Good shooting!" Ryan said, dropping back into his seat and starting the engine.

He throttled up to full speed, relieved that there had been no killing, and the earth moving machines lumbered toward town.

"I'm telling you it's suicide."

Klaus waved a hand toward the monitoring station. "We've got to do something. You can bet they've already called for help."

Chris wrinkled his forehead, searching for an alternative. "Wait a minute. What's in that shed at the bottom of the hill?"

"Mining supplies—piping, drills, explosives."

"Perfect."

Chris grabbed the laser rifle and made a semicircular path back toward the clearing. Klaus and the other two men followed, wondering what Chris had in mind. As soon as he could see the shed, he took aim and fired. The beam from the rifle bounced harmlessly off the wall of the shed and blew a small crater in the dirt. Laser fire from the top of the hill burned through the branches overhead, and Chris and the others threw themselves to the ground.

Klaus was annoyed. "It's ray-shielded!"

"I noticed. Looks like we'll have to use the door."

"How much time left?"

Chris checked his chronometer. "Two minutes. We gotta get inside that shed."

"Why?"

"I won't know till we get there."

Chris handed the rifle to one of the other men. "We're going to need some good cover."

The man nodded, took aim through the branches, and cut a blistering swath of laser fire up the wall of the monitoring station at the top of the hill. Neither of the guards dared to raise his head. Chris and Klaus cut across the clearing, pulled open the door to the shed, and threw themselves inside, closing the door behind them. Chris had not expected to find the door unlocked, and looking quickly around the room, he saw why.

"No explosives."

"What do you need explosives for?"

"I was hoping the concussion might set off the alarms. Do you still have the half pound of explosives?"

"Yes, but it's not enough."

"Maybe it doesn't have to be."

Chris picked up one of the drill bits and examined it, then grabbed a three-foot length of pipe. Dragging the point of the bit down the pipe, he was unable to make a scratch.

"Come on!" he urged.

He opened the door and stood back while a barrage of laser blasts ricocheted off the door. Answering fire came from the woods, and the guards were pinned down again. Chris and Klaus rolled out the door and pounded across the clearing, diving into the bushes.

Panting, Chris turned to Klaus. "I need your explosives, too."

Klaus reached into his pack with his good hand and pulled out a stick of reddish clay three inches long and an inch square. Chris pushed the stick into one end of the pipe.

"How do you set it off?"

"Heat in excess of one hundred fifty degrees."

Chris dropped the drill bit down the pipe, blunt end first, then rummaged in Klaus's pack and pulled out an incendiary. Klaus looked on with interest.

"Are you doing what I think you're doing?"

"It's our only chance. Which way is the Administration Building?" Klaus pointed diagonally behind them. "Get ready to run."

Finding a junction between two root systems at the base of a large tree, Chris set the incendiary for ten seconds, pressed it hard into the end of the pipe where the explosives were, and jammed the pipe between the roots. He took one second longer to aim the pipe above the monitoring station, then rushed behind the tree. The rest of the team was already face down, with their heads covered.

There was an ear-splitting roar as the explosives detonated. The drill bit whistled through the air like a bullet, punching a clean hole in the side of the dome. The horns on top of the monitoring station came vociferously to life, shrilling out a deafening *whoop! whoop! whoop!*

The guards at the top of the hill were too busy holding their ears to fire on the team's position, and Klaus led his team out of the area as fast as he could.

In the town square, Brice Maddock had personally overseen the stringing of the ropes, which were now ready to be placed over the heads of the five doomed prisoners. Three of them were cowering, much to Brice's satisfaction, but Tristan and his mother stood quite calmly, awaiting their fate. Brice could feel frustration rising like white heat in his face.

He paraded back and forth across the platform like a pompous dictator, regaining control over his anger, then ascended a podium he had ordered built specially for the occasion.

"Cursed is he who hangs from a tree! Today, we not only witness the punishment of five traitors, but I will reveal to you the most hideous betrayal of all. Perpetrated by my own blood, by none other than. . . ."

He never finished his sentence. The wail of the emergency horns echoed down the hillside and across the square, and the crowd was thrown into confusion. Two scrappers came roaring out of a side street, and people scattered in panic.

Guards scattered on the platform and around the square and fired on the scrappers. They were shocked to receive return fire. Two guards grabbed Brice and began hustling him toward the Detention Center for his protection, but he twisted and shouted to the others.

"Bring the prisoners! They must not be rescued!"

The prisoners were rounded up and the guards ran for the Detention Center. A laser bolt from the side of the square hit Ryan's companion, and he dropped his rifle, wounded in the arm. Asa's gunner opened up on the position of the guard responsible for the attack, and the guard turned and ran up an alley.

The last of the guards near the front of the square squeezed through the door of the Detention Center and slammed the door. Unaccustomed to being fired upon, the guards around the square were reluctant to fire, hoping someone else would take the lead. Ryan's scrapper lumbered to a stop with the shovel against the door and Asa rolled up behind, nearly pushing the first scrapper through the wall. The metal wall buckled but held, and Asa's team abandoned ship. With the crowd still trying to leave the area in panic, the guards in position around the square couldn't get a clear shot. Ryan seized the opportunity to stuff an armed incendiary into the engine compartment of his vehicle.

Then he grabbed his teammate and ducked into the nearest street. They paused just long enough to watch the scrapper go up in flames, before rounding the corner and slipping away.

When the alarm went off, the two guards in front of the Administration Building left their posts immediately to see what was happening. Nathan, Millie, and Amie ran across the open space, bounded up the stairs, and slipped through the front door.

Inside there was pandemonium. People flooded the hallways, frightened, bewildered, and angry. Nathan pulled his wife and daughter to one side.

"You know where the communications room is?" he whispered. Millie nodded. "I'm going to find Halton Maddock."

Nathan waded through the mass of people in the lobby and boarded an elevator. Millie grabbed Amie by the hand and ran down the hall. Everyone seemed to be trying to exit the building, but by holding hands and going single file, they were able to work their way against the traffic until they caught sight of the communications room. The guard by the door was studiously ignoring the thronging crowd of employees in the hallway. Millie bent down and spoke conspiratorially to her daughter.

"Think you can fake a broken arm?"

"Isn't that kind of like lying?"

"In this case, I think it's more like acting."

"Oh. Well, since you put it that way. . . ."

Amie took a deep breath and ran up the hallway, ready to put on an award-winning performance. Just in front of the guard, she tripped and went sprawling on the floor, taking several people down with her. As the guard stepped forward to help, Millie slipped in behind him and opened the door. The communications operator looked up from his console.

"Get out here, quick!" Millie barked.

The combination of the tangled bodies on the floor and the urgency in Millie's voice got the operator out of his seat. As he leaned out the door for a better look, Millie shoved him, hard. He stumbled forward and knocked the guard onto the pile of bodies. Millie closed the door and locked it.

She settled in easily at the console, paying no attention to the pounding and threats coming from the other side of the door.

Nathan found the sixth floor in as much confusion as the first. People were bustling to and fro, but no one seemed to know what to do. Nathan stopped person after frantic person, demanding the whereabouts of Halton Maddock. No one had seen him recently. His office was empty.

Finally, a man in a business suit shouted over his shoulder. "He's on the third floor, in ops."

Nathan ran down the hall to the elevators.

"That's right, a revolution on Venus!" Millie repeated. She hated dealing with bureaucrats.

The voice from Earth sounded bored. "How nice for you. Who is this?"

Outside the door, the pounding stopped.

"Lady! You stop transmitting right now, or I kill the little girl!"

Realizing that to make good on his threat, he'd better have a hand on the girl, the guard looked down. Amie wasn't there. He looked down the hallway and saw her squeezing through the crowded hallway.

"Hey, kid! Come back here!"

Inside the communications room, Millie heard the guard, smiled, and said "Good girl!" under her breath. Then she spoke into the microphone. "This is a transmission from Doctor Nathan Graham at SAFCOM, ID number seven one four, eee three kay six."

"Just a minute, I have to check this out," the voice said blandly.

Millie was livid. "I don't have a minute!"

There was no answer. Outside the door came the sound of a laser pistol being activated, and the door knob began to glow.

Nathan felt as if the elevator were taking forever and finally opted for the stairs. Taking three at a time, he reached the third floor in about a minute, and ran into yet another crowded hallway. He had a strong dislike for crowds, especially when he was in a hurry.

He grabbed a young fellow by the shoulders and yelled in his face. "Where's ops?"

The youthful employee's eyes widened and he pointed down the hallway. "Down the hall and to the right."

Nathan let him go and pressed through the crowd.

Millie was beginning to think all was lost when the voice came back on the line. "The ID checks out. What can I do for you?"

She resisted the urge to vilify the man with a few choice words from her pre-Christian days, and pulled a piece of paper from her pocket.

"Write this down. Call the Interstellar Trade Commission. Tell them the Maddock Mining Company, M–A–D–D–O–C–K, is in flagrant violation of contract one zero five one zero four, including illegal possession of mining rights, civil rights violations, slave labor, intimidation, unlawful imprisonment, kidnapping, and murder."

The door knob melted, and the door exploded inward. The force knocked Millie away from the console, and she screamed. The guard walked in, a look of unbridled fury on his face. He aimed his pistol at Millie's head, and Millie thought she was dead. As his finger tightened on the trigger, the voice came over the communicator again.

"Hey, lady! What's going on? Are you all right?"

The guard turned on the console viciously and burned a hole in it, then trained his gun on Millie again.

"Get out."

Nathan ran to a set of double doors and burst inside. He came to a sudden stop at the sight of a half dozen pistols pointed at his chest, and suddenly realized how wild and disheveled he must look. Halton Maddock looked up from the console he had been studying, shocked.

"Doctor Graham? But you're . . . I thought you were. . . ."

"Not yet. If you'll call your guards off for a moment, we need to talk."

CHAPTER 7

Amie found her way up to the sixth floor, looking for her father. But by the time she had completed the last flight of stairs, the halls were empty and most of the doors locked. She knocked on Halton Maddock's door but received no answer. Tears of frustration welled up in her eyes. She knew her mom needed help, but it looked like there was nothing she could do for her. If she asked too many questions, she could be caught or killed.

She wiped the tears from her eyes determinedly and walked down the hall a little further, stopping in front of Brice Maddock's office. She wanted to kick it, but knew that would accomplish nothing. The door was locked; the only visible mechanism was a thumb scanner beside the doorknob. Then she had an idea.

Reaching in her pocket, she pulled out a small kit that her father had given her for Christmas. It was a smaller version of the forensic kit he carried, but she had never expected to have an opportunity to use it. Inside was an assortment of tiny gadgets, tools, and capsules full of chemicals.

Amie applied a light dusting of powder from a tiny pouch to the doorknob and blew away the excess. There were fingerprints, clearly visible. She looked underneath the knob for a thumbprint and found one in remarkably good condition. Removing a square of gentle adhesive from her kit, she carefully

129

positioned it under the door knob and picked up the powdered thumbprint.

Gently Amie pressed the square against the scanner. The light from inside struck the adhesive and read the powder as Brice's thumbprint. The latch clicked, and Amie stepped inside and closed the door.

If Brice had anything incriminating in his office, it would be in a safe, she thought. A cursory search of the walls produced nothing, so she began looking around the desk for a secret button. Under the front of the desk, she found it. Holding her breath, she pressed it.

Across the room, a secret door popped open next to the bookcase. *Not a safe at all!* Relieved and terribly curious, Amie crossed the room and peered inside. A stairway wound downward, lit only by glowstrips. *This is probably stupid,* she thought to herself, *but I've got to find out where this leads. Lord, protect me.*

Grabbing onto the railing, Amie walked down into the darkness.

Nathan and the elder Mr. Maddock were face to face inside a utility closet off the operations center, so they could talk privately. At the moment, Halton was shaking his head.

"Brice has always been a fighter, but oppression and murder? I can't believe it."

"When was the last time you talked to the people?"

"We meet with Sammy Vile every week."

"Vile is working with Brice. I mean when is the last time you talked to anyone in town?"

"It's been . . . years." Halton looked surprised by the realization.

Nathan pressed the point. "Why has it been so long?"

"Well, it just seemed like something has always come up. Besides, I still have my weekly operations report."

"And who writes the report?"

Halton paused again. "Brice."

A raft of emotions passed over Halton's face, as he contemplated the unthinkable. Nathan did not want the man's natural affections to have a chance to cloud the issue, and pushed on.

"What about the hangings?"

"The Judas tree is for violent criminals. Law and order must be kept."

"And who decides when someone is worthy of death?"

"We have a magistrate, elected by the people."

"There is no magistrate. From what I have witnessed with my own eyes, Brice and the Seer serve as judge, jury, and executioner."

"Impossible."

"It may be happening right now."

"What do you mean?"

"Five innocent people were chosen at random and sentenced to hang at noon, unless I and my family are handed over to the authorities."

For the first time, Halton looked truly concerned. "We've got to stop this!"

"I was hoping you'd say that."

Halton had started for the door, but Nathan stopped him. "God willing, it has been postponed. If not, we are too late already. There is more at stake here than you realize."

He took the International Trade Commission document from his pocket and handed it to Halton. The older man began to read, noting with interest the signature of Terrence Maddock on the back. When he reached the section placing ownership of the mines in the hands of the people, he put down the paper in shock.

"You have been in violation of this agreement for over one hundred years," said Nathan.

Halton was silent, staring straight ahead. When he spoke again, he sounded as if his thoughts were far away. "What makes you think I won't destroy this document and hand you over to my guards?"

"I believe—I pray—that you are a man of integrity. But should you be otherwise, I have already sent a message to Earth informing the Trade Commission of the violation, and the conditions here."

Halton sighed and handed the document back to Nathan. "You needn't have worried. I may be blind where my son is concerned, but I am an honest man. At the moment, that trait is proving to be a terrible nuisance."

The interrogation room was small and sparsely furnished with only a table and two chairs. The light overhead cast an antiseptic glow on the bare walls, providing light without warmth, illumination without comfort.

Millie sat facing the only doorway, with her hands folded on the table. Between her and any chance of escape stood two armed guards, one by the door with weapon at ready and the other leaning over her menacingly, one foot planted on the other chair.

"For the last time, I want to know who you were talking to."

"Oh, very well. I don't see as it makes any difference now. I sent a message to the Interstellar Trade Commission."

"The what?"

"The Interstellar Trade Commission. It's an office on Earth that administers all off-world contracts."

"Why would you want to do a thing like that?"

"Because Brice Maddock is guilty of serious crimes against the colonists."

The guard jerked his foot down and slammed his fist against the wall. "Oh, that's great. Just great." He looked at Millie, half-apologetic, half-angry. "You're going to hang for this. I only hope he doesn't hang me with you. Come on."

He pulled Millie out of the chair and shoved her out the door, and the other guard fell in behind. They walked down the deserted hallway and out the front doors of the Administration Building. Millie was once again praying for deliverance.

No sooner were they down the trail and out of sight of the Administration Building, when the bushes came alive around them. Several hooded men surrounded them, some of them holding weapons. Millie recognized Klaus immediately but said nothing.

"Drop your guns, please," Klaus said, calmly.

The nearest guard grabbed Millie and pressed his gun into her back. "I'll kill her."

Klaus raised his laser rifle so that it was pointing at the guard's face, and the guard blanched. Beads of perspiration broke out on his forehead.

Klaus spoke evenly. "Do you really want your last act in this life to be the murder of an innocent woman? Drop your guns and live."

With a look of fear and anguish, the guards slowly lowered their weapons and dropped them to the ground. One of Klaus's men retrieved the weapons immediately, and Millie felt a hand on her shoulder.

"Mrs. Graham, I presume?"

"Chris!"

Mother and son embraced, and Klaus beamed unabashedly. Millie found her voice again. "Where's Ryan? Have you seen your father?"

"We don't know anything. We've been hiding out in the bushes since we set off the alarm. Several squads have gone past in both directions. I think we should go down to the square and see what's happening."

Millie looked at the two guards. "What do we do with these two?"

Klaus stepped out on the trail and addressed the guards matter-of-factly. "My friends, many changes are afoot, and we do not wish to be your enemies. I suspect Brice Maddock may not be with us much longer. If we are successful, you will be on the winning side. If we are not, we will be your prisoners."

The guards nodded cautiously, still not daring to believe they were escaping with their lives. Klaus turned and strode down the path as if he owned it, and the others fell in behind.

Millie watched him go for a moment before falling in step. "Not your average mine worker."

Chris smiled. "You can say that again."

When Amie reached the bottom of the stairs, she wasn't quite sure what to do next. The smooth, synthetic walls of the Administration Building had given way to rock, and the last three flights of steps were made of stone. Now the stairs had ended and she was faced with a blank stone wall.

Normally, she would have turned around and retraced her steps, but she had seen enough secret passages in the past few days that she was not about to give up easily. In the semidarkness it was difficult to see any detail on the wall. Feeling along with her fingertips, she systematically pressed anything that felt like an outcropping, until one of the rocks responded and a door swung open in the wall.

The stench from beyond nearly brought her to her knees, but she put a hand over her nose and began to breathe through her mouth. She debated whether or not to go in, both frightened and curious. But curiosity was stronger, and determinedly she stepped through the doorway.

The animal refuse on the floor did not alarm her—she had seen much worse working with her father. Some of the containers on the shelves looked dreadful, but their contents were unrecognizable, so all she felt was disgust. But suddenly she stopped. There was something else in the room—a presence. *Evil.*

The dull red light in the room seemed to go dim, and she felt as if the walls were beginning to close in. Thoughts of hopelessness flooded her mind. She was lost; she would not be found; she would never see the light of day again. A chill of stark terror raced through her, and she clasped her hands to her chest, calling out the one name she knew could save her.

"Jesus!"

The terror left her abruptly, and the light in the room seemed to grow brighter. The presence of evil was gone, and she felt peace and calm return. Amie no longer felt the urge to explore, and she walked toward the front of the cave to see if it might afford an easier exit.

Just as she neared the front entrance, there was a rustling and murmuring from the passage beyond. She stopped in her tracks. It was the Seer—Amie knew her immediately even though she had never laid eyes on her before—and the presence of evil had returned with her. Amie did know Saphirra was blind and hoped that by standing still, she might go unnoticed.

The hag was talking to herself. "Arrogant young fool! Can't even do a simple hanging. I ought to scratch his eyes out—"

The Seer stopped in mid-sentence and swung her head toward Amie. Amie resisted an impulse to scream.

Staring at her with the ghastly empty sockets of her eyes, the Seer spoke. "Lost our way, have we, dear?"

"You . . . you can see me!"

"Of course I can, darling girl." The words of affection oozed off her tongue like black oil, and the hag moved closer.

"I want to go home," Amie quavered.

"You are a long way from home, I'm afraid. There is good in you. I taste it like bile in my mouth, and it cannot be allowed to continue."

The hag reached out and Amie felt as if an icy hand had already closed around her throat. She cried out again.

"Jesus! Help me!"

The presence of evil left the room again, and the hag dropped to the floor, clutching her ears. "What have you done? My sight! My sight!"

Amie did not wait to see if the effect was temporary. She dashed out into the passage and ran as fast as she could. As the red glow from the cave fell behind, she suddenly found herself in darkness and slowed her pace. But the voice of the Seer spurred her onward.

"Come back here, you little vermin! You'll never escape! I can walk these passages with my eyes closed!"

The Seer broke into harsh laughter at her own joke. Amie stumbled once and then twice but didn't go down, always keeping a hand in front of her in case the passage should end. Several times, she thought she heard scuttling footsteps behind her, but the dreaded hand on her neck never came.

She had no idea where she was headed, but she kept going until her lungs ached with the effort. Her pace gradually slowed to a walk and she was fearing she would have to stop soon, when her hand brushed a small pipe. She stopped and groped with her other hand. There was another small pipe of the same length down below, and another the same distance above. *A ladder!*

She raced up the ladder as fast as she dared, waving her hand above with every other step to be sure she didn't bump her head. After thirty feet or so, her hand hit a hatch overhead. She fumbled with the latch, then threw the hatch open. Light streamed into the shaft from above, blinding her for a moment. Squinting against the brightness, she stepped gratefully out onto the grass and slammed the hatch shut.

The glade where she emerged ran downhill for fifty feet and into the woods. A hundred yards beyond, she could just make out the edge of town. She let out a little whoop of thanks and took off at a dead run.

By the time Klaus, Millie, Chris, and the others reached the town square, roving squads of security guards were busily restoring order. As soon as Asa's team had left the square, and all the shooting stopped, people began filtering back into the square, but there had been isolated reports of looting.

At the direction of several guards, a large contingent of towns-people was making an Olympian effort to clear the front of the Detention Center. There was no equipment heavier than the scrappers, so they had to set up a series of winches. Inch by aggravating inch, the machines were being dragged away from the door.

Klaus's group steered clear of the open areas and walked nonchalantly into the relative darkness of the shadows afforded by the eaves of a butcher shop at the back of the square. On the small porch they could observe the scene undetected. Chris scanned the area.

"I don't see any bodies. They must have made a clean get-away."

Millie sighed in exasperation. "That's your brother you're talking about, Chris. Bodies, indeed."

As they watched, the scrappers were finally pulled clear and the doors flew open. Brice Maddock was the first one out, his face a mask of outraged fury.

"I want the people responsible for this! Proceed with the hangings!"

For the second time that day, the five prisoners were led onto the platform and the nooses placed around their necks.

Chris tugged at Klaus's sleeve. "We've got to do something!"

"What do you suggest? The crowd is swarming with guards."

"A warning shot. Something—anything!"

"A shot would only alert the guards to our presence, and we would have ten hangings instead of five. I expected Nathan to be here by now. It looks like he failed."

Chris pressed his lips together in frustration. "We can't just stand here. We've got to do something!"

A gruff voice came from the ground beside the porch. "How about dropping your weapons and putting your hands in the air?"

They whirled to find two guards with weapons drawn. The air around them was thick with tension. Chris bit his lip, moving instinctively closer to his mother to shield her. Then the tableau was broken by a familiar voice.

"Excuse me?"

The guards whirled around and found themselves under the point of Ryan's laser rifle, trained on them from the roof of the next building. Klaus and Chris moved quickly to disarm them. Chris looked up at Ryan and grinned.

"Hey, little brother. What are you doing up there?"

"Dad never showed up, so Asa and I decided we better find a place with a view to wait it out."

"Where's Asa?"

"Across the square somewhere. I don't know."

"Well, unless somebody has a plan, five innocent people are going to die. You don't have one, do you?"

"Sorry," Ryan said, climbing over the edge and dropping to the street.

Klaus talked quickly to the two guards he had drafted on the trail, instructing them to fill in their two comrades in the interest of avoiding any further unpleasantness. The four guards huddled and started into a heated discussion, and Chris kept a gun on them just in case.

Across the square, Asa braced his rifle on the wooden rail surrounding the roof where he stood, and took aim at the bottom branch of the Judas tree. Brice was still striding back and forth across the platform, shouting at the crowd.

"Let this be a lesson to you! Resistance is useless!"

He walked over to his first victim, a middle-aged, bearded man with frightened eyes. Brice lashed out savagely with his foot, kicking the supporting block out from under him. Simultaneously, Asa fired and a bolt of energy tore along the length of the bottom branch, severing all the ropes. The man landed in a sitting position, a look of shock on his face. Then everything happened at once.

Brice shouted orders at his guards, and a devastating barrage of laser fire saturated Asa's position. As if in response to the laser fire, Nathan Graham and Halton Maddock appeared from the alley that led to the tube car loading dock and ran onto the platform. Nathan grabbed Brice roughly by the lapels, silencing him, and Halton gave the order to cease fire. The guns gradually fell silent. The corner of the building where Asa had last been seen was now reduced to a river of molten slag.

A hush fell over the crowd of townspeople, even as each person nudged his or her neighbor and the word spread that this was Halton Maddock. Many of them had never seen him in person, and craned to get a better view of this man who could spawn a monster like Brice. The slightly disheveled but distinguished gentleman in a business suit was not at all what they expected. Halton addressed the crowd from Brice's podium.

"I am Halton Maddock. Let me begin by saying I have been away too long." He glanced darkly at Brice. "I fear you have not been well served in my absence. There are many matters that must be resolved, but I promise you things will be different from now on."

There were murmurs both of approval and skepticism, and someone yelled, "How different? What proof do you offer?"

"I have a document that says the mining operations belong to the people!"

A ripple of shock passed through the crowd. Halton was pleased with the effect, and he continued. "That's right. All mining operations belong to you the townspeople, the descendants of the original colonists."

The voice of the Seer rose over the noise of the crowd. "He lies! It's a trick!"

The crowd parted in fear, to allow the Seer to approach. She climbed the steps to the platform and glared at Brice. "You imbecile! You could have had it all. Now we're going to do it my way, and you will serve me!"

"You're out of your mind," Brice sneered.

The Seer snarled with such ferocity that Brice took a step backward. "Silence!"

The crowd was so hushed you could hear a pin drop, and Halton spoke. "Saphirra, I don't know what kind of schemes you've been cooking up in your twisted mind, but I'm only going to say this once. Go home. *Now.*"

She grinned her hideous grin. "Halton Maddock, I could kill you for that, but you are only a hapless pawn in the sociopathic machinations of your son."

"It's a lie! She's crazy! I don't even know the woman!" Brice spluttered.

"Whatever he has done, he is still my son. And I am in charge here."

Saphirra laughed unpleasantly. "Blind fool. Do you really doubt . . . ?" She turned to the crowd. "Do any of you doubt that I could kill you with a wave of my hand?"

Horrified silence reigned for a moment, and then Nathan faced the Seer. "I do."

Saphirra turned in surprise, but her face showed no sign of comprehension. "Who said that? Who dares?"

"I am Nathan Graham."

The Seer recoiled at the name. "Why is it that I cannot see you?"

"Because my Master is stronger than yours."

She knew what he said was true, and she shuddered. "Leave us alone! We have a right to be here!"

Brice could feel the situation slipping from his grasp. In a last ditch attempt to retain control, he yelled at the guards on the platform.

"Hang them! Hang them all!"

The guards reacted reflexively to Brice's voice and grabbed Nathan, Halton, and the Seer, dragging them toward the Judas tree. Saphirra was kicking and screaming.

"You fools! He's the one who should be hung! He's been planning to murder his father and take over the company!"

These new accusations stopped the guards in their tracks. Saphirra cackled, pleased at the effect of her words.

"I should know. I was his accomplice."

Nathan leaned toward Halton and spoke in a whisper. "If you're going to take command, now's the time. Halton?"

But Halton wasn't listening. He was staring straight ahead with a look of grief on his face. Until now, he had hoped the worst of the allegations against his son were not true. "My son . . ."

Brice clenched his fists, and his face flushed hotly. "That's outrageous! She's insane!"

The guards were not convinced.

"String her up! That's an order!"

The guards didn't move.

"It's a lie, I tell you!"

A young voice came clear and true from the front of the crowd.

"It's not a lie," Amie said, with as much courage as she could muster. "There's a secret passage from your office down to the Seer's cave. I've seen it."

Brice's mouth dropped open.

"Would you care to explain that?" Nathan addressed Brice for the crowd.

"I don't have to explain anything! I'm still in charge here!"

Halton shook his head sadly. "No, you're not, Brice. You're under arrest."

The color drained from Brice's face, even as in the crowd shock gave way to rage. Brice sensed the growing animosity of the crowd and lunged sideways, tearing a laser rifle from the hands of one of the guards. He aimed it at his father, and every other weapon on the platform pointed right back at him.

"Keep away. Keep away, or I'll burn him down."

Brice backed down the platform steps, and the crowd parted to let him pass. He held the guards at bay until he reached the corner of the street. Then he broke and ran for the tube car platform. Someone in the crowd yelled, "Get him!" and with a roar, the mob was after him. Halton ordered the guards not to interfere, then sat down on the platform steps in misery.

Brice thundered across the tube car loading dock, heart pounding, and jumped into the nearest tube car. As the mob rounded the corner, Brice cut a swath across the front row with his laser rifle, and four men doubled over, clutching their chests. Far from slowing them down, this new outrage only fueled the fury of the mob.

He hit the button for the Administration Building and the start button, and the canopy dropped into place. The car reached the tunnel just ahead of the leading fringe of the mob, and took off.

"He's headed for the Administration Building! Come on!"

Back in the square, the security squads were standing around like sheep without a shepherd, along with many of the townspeople who had declined to join the mob. Millie ran to Amie's side, and Nathan jumped down from the platform and put his arms around them both. In all the confusion, Saphirra Kraal hurried off the platform and vanished into the crowd.

Chris and Ryan were about to join the rest of the family when the mob swept back through the square and up the street toward the Administration Building. Klaus put his hand on

Chris's shoulder. "Those guards on the platform are still holding their guns. We'd better get up there before somebody snaps."

Chris and Ryan ran to the front of the square and were received by their parents with open arms. Klaus sent his men to check on the welfare of Asa, then made his way to the platform. "You!" he ordered, assuming a new air of authority. "Drop your weapons."

Klaus's voice snapped Halton back to reality, and he stood up, eyeing the newcomer shrewdly.

"Who are you?"

"Klaus Darmon, sir. One of your miners."

"Not anymore. Now I work for you."

Nathan walked quickly to the platform. "Halton, that mob has gone after your son. If they catch him, they'll kill him. If they don't, there may be mass murder in the Administration Building."

"You're right." Halton turned to the guards on the platform. "We're not out of this yet. Bring your guns and come with me."

Nathan handed him the Trade Commission document. "You'd better take this."

"Right."

Nathan started to follow, but Millie grabbed him by the arm. "You're not going up there?"

"He may need a mediator." Nathan hurrried to catch Halton's group.

A shout went up from the rubble of the nearby building. Klaus's men had found Asa, just barely alive. There was a flurry of activity as Klaus rushed over to supervise the rescue of his dear friend. When they had formed a makeshift stretcher and carried him off to the medical center, Klaus returned to the square, obviously deeply concerned. Trying to shake off his anxiety, he glanced around the square. Then his expression changed to one of alarm.

"Where's the hag?"

Chris scanned the square. "Long gone, by the look of it."

Klaus turned to Amie. "She must not escape! You said you found a secret way into the Seer's lair?"

Amie nodded.

"Show me!"

Klaus and Amie set out after Nathan, leaving Millie, Chris, and Ryan staring at each other. Millie exhaled in exasperation and started walking, calling over her shoulder as she went. "Well, don't just stand there, come on."

Brice's tube car came to a stop in the Administration Building. As he ran for the elevator, the first wave of the mob neared the front door. Gasping for breath, he pulled out a key and stuck it in the emergency service slot. The elevator took him straight to the sixth floor, while the lobby downstairs filled with the angry mob.

The elevator doors opened and he ran for his father's office. But the quickest of the mob were already in the hallway.

"There he is!"

Brice made it through the door and slammed it locked, just ahead of the angry mob. He ran over to his father's wall safe, while the men outside began trying to break the door down. There were important documents and Halton's ID card, both of which he would need if he was going to make any claim of ownership when he reached Earth.

Brice was still trying to remember the combination to the safe when the door began to give way. He swore under his breath and headed for his father's emergency exit. As he ran down the first flight of stairs, he heard the door in his father's office break open and the sound of angry shouts.

Brice reached the bottom of the steps and started toward an outside door, but stopped suddenly. He could hear the sounds of the mob on the grounds outside. The group on the stairway was nearly down. He was trapped. Or was he? There was a single tube car here, sitting on a track all its own. Above it was posted a placard which read, IN CASE OF FIRE, DO NOT USE.

Brice jumped into the car and pressed the button for the launch bay. Perhaps he would have time to force a launch somehow. Surely the crew hadn't heard about the rioting in the dome.

143

He pressed the green button and the canopy closed and locked into place.

The first few members of the mob reached the bottom of the stairs and ran to the car, beating on it with their fists. Brice leaned back in his seat. He knew he was safe. There was no way for them to break in. He took a deep breath and opened his eyes to see the engraved name on the brass plaque on the dashboard: *Halton Maddock*.

Brice screamed.

Beneath the tube car, the device he had ordered Lormock to install was activated, overriding the failsafe on the inside of the track and engaging the purge circuits on the far side of the dome. The tube car shot into the tunnel, accelerating to a hundred miles an hour in a few seconds. Mercifully, the force of the acceleration knocked Brice unconscious.

The car roared downhill, curving to the right past the town, through the tunnel, and past the point where Amie's car had been destroyed a few days earlier. A thousand feet from the side of the dome, the car left the main tube, roared up the ejector chute, and blasted out of the dome, arcing several hundred feet over the face of the mountainside, before dashing to pieces on the rocks below.

After Brice's apparent escape from the Administration Building, as Nathan predicted, the mob began tearing the place apart. Several squads of security guards had surrendered, only to be severely beaten at the hands of the outraged townspeople. They had been at the mercy of the company for as long as any of them could remember, and now a lifetime of rage was being poured out within the confines of the building.

Part of the mob spilled out into the garden, and as they looked around at the high walls with barbed wire on top, they fell strangely silent. Here was a place of astonishing beauty; yet it was a symbol of the separation and favoritism practiced by the company. One of the men carrying a wooden club walked over to a bed of azaleas and raised his club, as if to crush them to pieces. Before he could bring the club down, one of his comrades placed a steady hand on his shoulder.

"'Tis the walls that should come down, not the flowers."

The tension in the man's muscles never waned, as he looked up from the flower bed toward the high wall. With an animal howl, he charged the wall, and began beating on it with his club. The others joined in with reckless abandon, pounding on the walls with anything they could get their hands on—sticks, rocks, metal posts—or their hands when nothing useful could be found.

When Halton reached the front of the Administration Building with his contingent of security guards, he stopped for a minute, trying to figure out what to do. The townspeople gathered outside had been unable to squeeze in through the front doors, for the ground floor was jammed with people. Some of them were pounding on the walls, but others milled about aimlessly, as if beginning to wonder what they were doing there.

Halton walked up to the group out front and shouted at the top of his lungs.

"Listen to me! What I said down in the square was true! All the mining operations on Venus belong to you! All of it! This document proves it! Do you hear what I'm saying? You are destroying your own property!"

Wading into the crowd, he kept yelling the same message again and again, waving the Interstellar Trade agreement over his head. The crowd parted to let him through, and he pushed his way through the front doors, still hollering his simple sermon of ownership. Nathan followed him inside, then stood off to one side to watch. Apparently Halton was getting along just fine without a mediator.

Every person within earshot, even the ones in the process of violently expressing their anger, gradually fell silent. Hushed whispers and murmurs spread like wildfire through the mob, and several groups began taking Halton's message to the other floors.

With the general cessation of hostilities inside the Administration Building, Klaus and Amie were able to forge a path to the elevators. Millie, Chris, and Ryan piled in after them, and the elevator started upward. From across the lobby, Nathan saw them going into the elevator, but the noise was such that yelling was pointless.

Inside the elevator, the sudden quiet was such a surprise the Grahams and Klaus felt uncomfortable. The only sound was their own breathing. The doors opened to the top floor, which was crowded but passable nonetheless, and Amie led the way to Brice's office.

The door was still locked, and before Amie could explain how she let herself in the first time, Klaus kicked it in. Amie ran around behind the desk and pressed the secret button that opened the hidden doorway. Chris gave her a congratulatory grin, and followed Klaus through the door and down the stairs. Not about to be left out, Amie scooted around the desk and slipped through the door ahead of Ryan, with Millie taking up the rear.

On the chance that Saphirra was in her lair, they tiptoed down the steps trying to make as little noise as possible. In the dark at the bottom, Klaus produced a torch, then Amie showed him the rock which served as the latch for the door and moved out of the way. Klaus pressed on the rock, and the door swung open.

As before, the stench was nearly overpowering, but they stepped into the dark room beyond without hesitation. The light of Klaus's torch illuminated the Seer's lair better than it had been since it was cut by the original stonemasons. Frozen in the act of packing a canvas bag beside her bed, Saphirra stood gaping at her unwelcome visitors.

"Leave me be! I am just an old woman!"

Klaus walked further into the room, stopping beside a vile altar. "You have much to answer for, Saphirra."

The hag raised her hands, claws extended. "Stay back! Do you think I am powerless?"

As if swept aside by some tremendous, unseen hand, Klaus was flung backwards, landing in a heap at Chris's feet. The

Grahams gathered around their fallen comrade, checking for injuries, while Saphirra continued to rant and rave.

"I am god here! You will worship me!"

Klaus sat up on his elbows, looking perplexed, and not a little frightened. "How did she do that?"

Millie put a comforting hand on his shoulder. "Don't try to get up. She has given herself over to the Enemy. He is powerful. You must trust the Lord for His protection."

"But how can we fight against such power?" Klaus asked, fearing the answer.

Amie stood up and squared her shoulders, walking slowly toward the hag, looking evenly into the blank, staring eyes. "With a word."

"Amie! Get back here!" Millie hissed.

It was too late. Amie had already passed the altar and was nearly face to face with the hag. Saphirra turned her head toward Amie for the second time that day, and this time there was fear behind her eyes. The hag started shaking, but Amie was determined not to look away.

"Who are you?"

"We are the Queen of Darkness! Weee ruuullle heeerrre!" the hag shrieked.

Amie squinted against the force of the hag's tirade, but she was determined.

"By whose authority?"

The hag convulsed, bit her tongue until it bled, but said nothing.

Amie was angry, sick of the corruption wrought by this fallen creature. "By whose authority!"

"By Azrael, the demon spirit of death! Now leave us alone! You have no right!"

"You're wrong. By the authority of Jesus Christ, I command you to leave this woman alone. Get out of here! Get out!"

At the name of Jesus, the hag clutched her head, and dropped to her knees. All around the hag's chamber, shelves collapsed and tables were overturned, as if the forces of Light and Darkness were fighting a pitched battle in the room. Millie grabbed her sons' hands.

"Pray!"

They began praying out loud, shouting over the din of clattering pottery and breaking glass. The light in the room seemed to grow brighter for a moment, and over the noise of battle and the prayers of her family, Amie began to sing.

"Jesus loves me, this I know, for the Bible tells me so . . ."

While Chris and Ryan continued to pray, Millie joined in the song.

". . . little ones to Him belong, they are weak but He is strong! Yes, Jesus loves me! Yes, Jesus loves me! Yes, Jesus loves me, the Bible tells me so!"

At Amie's feet, the hag thrashed and shook briefly and then was still. The noise around the room grew louder for a moment, then stopped as suddenly as it had started. Chris helped Klaus to his feet and they all moved to Amie's side. Saphirra lay curled up on the floor, a frail old woman, motionless except for the steady rise and fall of her breath.

Klaus looked at the devastation around the room, then down at the vanquished Queen of Darkness.

"Our God is an awesome God."

In the Administration Building, Halton had managed to convince the mob to return to the square. Nathan enlisted the help of several strong young men to begin carrying the wounded to the medical center and suggested to any employee who would listen that he or she join the crowd, as this affected them as well. The mixture of people wandering out of the front doors toward town was unique to say the least. Peasants and workers in rags walked beside executives in business suits, many of them for the first time in their lives. The only thing each person shared with all the others was a dazed expression over the latest turn of events.

With the crowds in the hallways beginning to thin, Nathan hurried upstairs to check on the whereabouts of his family. His best guess was that they had gone to the top floor, maybe to

Halton's office. At the top floor, he jogged down the hall toward the president's office, and nearly ran into Millie coming out of Brice's office, followed by Ryan and Amie.

Nathan was about to ask them what they were doing, when Chris and Klaus emerged with the semiconscious form of Saphirra between them. "What happened to her?" Nathan asked, amazed.

Millie gave her husband a tired, patient look. "We'll tell you later."

CHAPTER 8

Although some of the employees were badly beaten in the riot, no one was killed in the violence at the Administration Building. Asa, though burned over thirty percent of his body, was proving once again to have an incredible constitution. Mining operations were temporarily suspended, pending critical negotiations between the townspeople and the company. Saphirra, Sammy Vile, and several members of the security force were locked up in the Detention Center during the first few hours of the revolution, as the townspeople were calling it, mostly for their own protection. Many enemies had been made during the years of oppression, and there were a fair number of townspeople who were not ready to forgive or forget.

Nathan offered his services as a neutral third party to mediate between the various interested parties. The first meetings were tense, but the representatives from both sides were sufficiently shell shocked to be ready to make some concessions.

Two weeks after the revolution, an Interplanetary Police Force troop transport landed in the launch bay. Before the bay was closed, the ship disgorged a dozen strike teams, wearing environment suits and ready for a fight. Based on the severity of the message Millie had sent to Earth, the commander had decided he better take the colony by surprise. They had maintained communicator silence once they were in orbit around Venus, despite several attempts to hail them from the colony.

They were preparing to blow the main doors to the tube car loading bay when the launch bay finished repressurizing, and the doors opened on their own. Instead of a battalion of crazed colonists brandishing weapons, the strike teams were greeted by three nicely dressed men and a woman. Even more surprising to the commander, this little group did not seem the least bit disturbed to be staring down the sights of several dozen laser rifles.

After thorough examination of the tube car loading bay by his force, the commander stepped forward.

"Commander Weaver, Third Battalion, McKinley Station, responding to a message received by the Interstellar Trade Commission two weeks ago."

Millie extended her hand. "Millie Graham. I sent the message."

"So where's the disaster?"

Nathan stepped forward. "I'm Doctor Nathan Graham. Forgive the confusion. When the message was sent, the colony was in the throes of revolution. We would have told you if you had answered our hail, but I suppose you had to maintain radio silence."

The commander was beginning to look exasperated. "Are you telling me this whole trip was for nothing?"

"Not at all. The rioting is over, but the peace is still shaky. We have an armed security force that up until two weeks ago served a totalitarian government. Some of the guards still aren't sure who they're supposed to take orders from. We will need your help to keep the peace while we dismantle the security force and replace it with people from the colony."

Some of the IPF officers began to relax a little, and the commander turned to his second in command. "Secure from general quarters. Tell the SI and ITC civs they're on deck."

The strike force sent to Venus in response to Millie's message included contingents of civilians from the Office of Social Infrastructure and the Interstellar Trade Commission, experts trained in the repair and maintenance of societies, especially colonies. Despite Nathan's assurances, the commander was not sanguine

151

about sending his troops to the main dome one at a time in the tube cars. Once several IPF officers were through, and met no resistance, he began to consider the possibility of relaxing.

The townspeople eyed the IPF officers suspiciously at first, wondering if they weren't exchanging one oppressive security force for another. But the members of the strike force proved to be tough, courteous, experienced, and unwaveringly strict with anyone who didn't comply with the temporary regulations instigated by Halton Maddock and Nathan Graham the day after the mob stormed the Administration Building.

For their part, the old security force behaved themselves, as most of them longed to leave Venus and make a new start on Earth now. Their weapons were confiscated, along with their uniforms, so there would be no question about who was in authority. Based on testimony from some of the townspeople, a few of the guards were jailed until a court could be convened.

Social reconstruction was one of the more complicated disciplines, made more difficult by the fact that there was little opportunity to practice in live situations. There were only a half dozen colonies in the solar system, and most of those were well established. The fall of the government on Venus was an unusual event, to say the least, and an optimal situation for the social infrastructure specialists who had arrived with the strike force.

Once the security functions were well in hand, the commander assigned several of his officers the task of investigating what had transpired prior to their arrival. Nathan, Klaus, and Halton joined the officers in a conference room and weren't heard from again for the better part of a day. The commander had told his officers not to set foot out of that room without a report and a list of suspects and witnesses, and they knew—from unpleasant past experience—that he meant it.

Elsewhere in the main dome, the social infrastructure team quickly found the number of people they had brought was woefully inadequate for the task of rebuilding the colony. Mine workers were assigned to various construction teams, and Millie, Chris, Ryan, and Amie were drafted to help with the building of schools, training of teachers, and construction of better housing in the town.

It was only a few days later that Amie sat in one of the new classrooms off Main Street with a woman almost old enough to be her mother. The smell of fresh building materials was strong but not unpleasant, and the room was actually starting to look like a school. Rows of desks, unloaded from the IPF ship and painstakingly sent one by one via the tube cars, sat waiting for the students who would begin classes over the next several months. Computers were mounted in the tops of the desks, and the seats were large enough to accommodate the adults who would be among the first students.

The chair in which Amie sat was a little rickety, and not very clean, as it had been borrowed from a shop across the street. The woman sat at one of the desks, learning to use the machine she would eventually be teaching others to use. She had grasped the mechanics of English without much difficulty, but math was proving to be a challenge.

"Eight times six?"

The woman furrowed her brow. "Fifty-six?"

"Close. Think of it like sixteen times three."

"Sixteen . . . thirty-two . . . forty-eight?"

"Right! Bring up the grid. See? Eight times seven is fifty-six."

The lesson was interrupted a moment later, when Chris leaned in the door. His hair was a mess, his sleeves rolled up to his elbows, and smudges of grime and grease adorned his clothes from top to bottom.

"Hey, squirt."

"Nice outfit. What have you been doing?"

"I spent most of the day trying to fix the engine on that front-end loader Ryan burned up. He did a pretty thorough job of it, but I think most of the parts can be replaced from the IPF ship's stores, or manufactured." Chris loved it whenever he got a chance to use his engineering skills to help out someone in need—almost as much as he enjoyed talking about his accomplishments. "Our construction crew is getting ready to break ground on some new houses along the edge of town. Ryan's got his own crew clearing away some of the lighter stuff right now. He's not a bad foreman, for a runt."

Amie was eager to get back to the lesson, and her impatience began to show. "Sounds great."

"Yeah, but that's not why I stopped by. There's going to be a hearing in the third floor auditorium in the Administration Building starting at sixteen hundred hours. Dad says you need to be there."

"Okay."

"Where's Mom?"

"Two streets over, teaching a class. Across from the boot shop, I think."

"Thanks." Chris nodded to the woman. "Don't let her push you too hard."

The Grahams returned to their old suite in the Administration Building after the hearing late in the day exhausted but encouraged. It was only the first round of many to come, but it had gone well. As they each found a comfortable spot to relax, they couldn't help feeling a little guilty about their luxurious surroundings, now that they knew how many of the colonists lived. They were all feeling a little numb. This trip had certainly not turned out the way any of them thought it would.

Nathan settled into a comfortable chair at a synthetic wooden desk, pulling a pocket computer from his inside jacket pocket. The day had been long already, but he knew he had to get the last of his thoughts down while they were still fresh. Otherwise he would hate himself when it came time to write his report.

Chris lounged in a corner of the sofa and eyed his brother at the other end. There is a unique quality to brotherhood—a peculiar, nearly irresistible impulse to interact physically and aggressively, particularly if the attack is unprovoked and guaranteed to irritate. For no apparent reason, Chris made a fist and punched his brother in the leg.

Ryan reacted with tired outrage, falling immediately into the old patterns, "Ow! You big musk ox!"

154

Chris offered the appropriate answer. "Ooooh, did Runty-Wunty boom his leg?"

Millie was almost too tired to object, but when Ryan surprised his brother with a headlock, she decided to stop the altercation before they broke some of the furniture. "Boys! Not now, please."

Ryan let his brother go, and they retreated to opposite ends of the sofa, straightening their clothes as they went. Chris gave Ryan an admiring look.

"Not bad. We must try that again some time."

Ryan rubbed his leg, scowling, "Right. Next time, I'll start if you don't mind."

Nathan finished his data entry and joined his wife at the coffee table. He looked around at his family, and despite his fatigue, felt a surge of pride for every one of them.

"I want to take a moment to thank you all. When I first talked about this trip, I made it sound like a walk in the park. You have all been wonderful. I don't think I heard a single complaint the whole time."

Chris shrugged. "It seems to be turning out okay."

Nathan was not so sure. "I think it's going to be touch and go for a while. Halton needs to do something to win the confidence of the townspeople."

"How about a party?" Ryan quipped.

Chris smiled. "Right. They'd string him up from that tree in the middle of town."

"Daddy, why did they call it the Judas tree?"

"I'm not sure, Amie. I suppose because Judas Iscariot betrayed Jesus."

Ryan frowned. "But the people didn't know the Bible. Where did they get the name?"

"The tree was named by Saphirra's mother," Millie interjected. "If Catherine Josiah had trained her, that might explain it."

"What do you think really happened to Catherine?" Chris asked.

Nathan thought for a long time, and the others were silent. When he finally spoke, he looked grieved.

"They probably killed her. I can't imagine her keeping quiet in exile, even if they threatened her. But we'll probably never know."

Amie looked crestfallen. "How sad!"

"If I'm right about that, she died doing the Lord's work. I can't think of a better way to go."

Nathan stood up and stretched, ready to change the subject. "We'll probably be leaving in a few days. The commander says he has guest quarters available on board. I'm sure it's nothing fancy, but it can only be better than the trip over."

Chris stood up and started toward his bedroom.

"If anyone wants me, I'll be in the shower for the next forty-eight hours."

Nathan was awakened the next morning by the sound of the front door call tone. He threw on a robe and shuffled to the door, yawning all the way. The thought of some new disaster was almost more than he could take right now.

He pressed the button and the door slid open, revealing the beaming face of Klaus.

"What brings you here so early?" Nathan said, genuinely pleased.

Klaus was all business. "Get the family together, Nathan! Come to the garden."

Without further explanation, he was gone. Bewildered, Nathan roused the others and they dressed quickly, agreeing to eat breakfast after whatever momentous event was happening in the garden. Millie and Amie led the way, remembering their earlier adventure.

This time, the garden was packed with people, both from the town and the Administration Building. No one seemed to know what was going on. Klaus spoke to the Grahams as if sharing some grand secret.

"The elder Mr. Maddock and I dreamed this up late last night."

As if on cue, Halton Maddock appeared at the front of the

crowd. He looked as if he were about to make a speech, then thought better of it and hollered over the wall.

"Go ahead, Lee!"

From outside the walls came the sound of engines starting. And then the walls came tumbling down. As huge chunks of concrete tangled with barbed wire fell in a cloud of shards and dust, the people from the town let out a cheer. Halton had been right to forego his speech. Nothing more needed to be said.

After a full morning of hearings, Ryan decided to pay another visit to Asa in the medical center. Though the laser burns had indeed been terrible, Asa's recuperative powers were unusually strong. And not to be minimized was the fact that nearly everyone in the Brotherhood along with the Graham family had been praying for him.

Ryan walked up beside the gentle giant's bed and waited for him to open his eyes. Asa's body was still wrapped from neck to waist with treated bandages, and although he opened his eyes, he didn't turn his head.

"What brings you here again, Ryan Graham?" Asa asked softly.

"I came to visit a dear friend."

Even breathing was painful, but Asa wouldn't show it. "I heard about Brice."

"He brought it on himself. Hey, that was some great shooting at the square."

Asa gritted his teeth against the pain. "It was not without some cost."

"Why don't you take something for the pain?"

"Pain builds character."

Ryan leaned close and lowered his voice, so as not to injure his friend's pride. "A body can only take so much character."

"Perhaps. Has there been any more fighting?"

"I don't think so. The security force is all ready to ship back to Earth. Sammy Vile and Saphirra are in custody. They found the man who sabotaged the car that killed Brice, somebody named Lormock, I think. The walls around the garden are down. Some of the company employees are having a difficult time adjusting, but not to the point of shedding blood."

"I talked to Tristan this morning. Some members of the Brotherhood are having the same difficulty. It feels as if we have been at war for several lifetimes. You can't just turn it off."

Ryan stood up straight. "If you're going to make this thing work, you're all going to have to try."

Epilogue

Hearings dragged on for several days, but the only additional arrests were two or three members of the former security force. With the hearings out of the way, negotiations between the colony and the company began in earnest. Because he was in some sense a victim of his son's crimes, Halton Maddock retained his position as president of the company. When it was time for the townspeople to elect a representative for the negotiations, the people named Klaus Darmon because of his part in both the revolution and the subsequent investigation.

Saphirra Kraal and Sammy Vile were formally charged with conspiracy to commit murder, and Benton Lormock was charged with manslaughter. As preparations were made for the demobilization of the strike force, the IPF threw all three in the brig on their heavy cruiser—along with the other prisoners from the former security force—to face trial on Earth. Two dozen volunteers from town were trained as the new security force, but they would be referred to ever after as domestic police, with the chief reporting to Halton and Klaus.

With additional social reconstruction teams already en route from Earth, the Grahams loaded most of their luggage into the guest quarters on the IPF cruiser, which was scheduled to leave in two days. While Nathan wound down his participation in the ongoing negotiations, Chris and Ryan continued to assist with construction of new housing in town. Millie and Amie pressed on with the social reconstruction crew to assemble a curriculum for the schools that would soon be opening to the general public.

The *Mother Lode* was cleared to resume ore shipments to Earth, and the Grahams all bid a fond farewell to Captain Fairborne. Belatedly, the commander of the IPF contingent showed up just before takeoff to present him with a citation for his bravery in helping Ryan escape.

On the afternoon of the day of departure, the Grahams left the Administration Building for the last time and took one more ride in the tube cars to the launch bay. They were met just inside the main door of the launch bay by Halton, Klaus, and Asa (who amazingly was on his feet) while a host of technicians and cargo specialists made final preparations for liftoff.

Nathan shook Halton's hand. "Thank you, Halton. It's been . . . interesting."

"No—thank *you*. None of this would have happened if your family hadn't come here. The workers are happy, and you wouldn't recognize the town anymore. Since the people assumed ownership of the mines, production is up seventeen percent."

"Don't let them bully you," Nathan said, smiling.

Halton laughed.

Chris shook hands with Klaus. "You take care of yourself."

"I'll be fine. The president here says once I learn the ropes, I might make a good chief operating officer."

Ryan held out a hand to Asa, remembering that under his robe he was still covered in bandages. "Hope you feel better."

Asa slapped Ryan on the back jovially, knocking the wind out of him. "Have a safe trip, Ryan Graham."

Klaus addressed his friends from Earth. "You're part of our family for life, y'know. Our first church service is on Sunday. Sorry you won't be here. You will have to come see us again sometime."

The Grahams walked up the ramp onto the IPF cruiser, and the three men on the floor of the launch bay walked out the main doors into the observation lounge. As the engines ignited, and the ship rose up out of the dome, Halton smiled bemusedly.

"I'm really sorry to see them go."

"Not to worry. They'll be back," Klaus said, watching the ship grow smaller against the pale sky.

"What makes you so sure, Mr. Darmon?"

Klaus looked at Halton and grinned.

"Nathan's company still needs a booster station."

The first three books in the Perimeter One Adventures series are available at your local Christian bookstore.

The Misenberg Accelerator (Book One)

When Dr. Nathan Graham is invited to a symposium at the Perimeter One space station, his entire family teeters on the brink of danger. While exploring the station, the Grahams reunite with an old friend and an old enemy who could seriously alter their vacation plans.

The SHONN Project (Book Two)

As an assistant in the formation of SHONN, a learning, thinking machine, Chris dedicates a considerable amount of time to the project. But when the machine is found to be an agent for crime, Chris becomes one of its innocent targets.

Out of Time (Book Three)

The Grahams learn the hard way that time really does have a way of flying. When a rookie time experiment goes awry at the New Denver Technology Center, the Grahams are the unlucky victims in a race against the clock.